# CHECKED

## GOLD HOCKEY #7

## ELISE FABER

CHECKED
BY ELISE FABER
Newsletter sign-up

CHECKED
Copyright © 2020 Elise Faber
Print ISBN-13: 978-1-946140-36-4
Ebook ISBN-13: 978-1-946140-50-0
Cover Art by Jena Brignola

# GOLD HOCKEY SERIES

# Gold Cast of Characters

**H**eroes and Heroines:

*Brit Plantain (Blocked)* — first female goalie in the NHL, loves boy bands

*Stefan Barie (Blocked)* — captain of the Gold

*Sara Jetty (Backhand)* — artist and figure skater

*Mike Stewart (Backhand)* —defenseman for the Gold, romance guru

*Blane Hart (Boarding)* — center for the Gold, number 22

*Mandy Shallows (Boarding)* — trainer and physical therapist

*Max Montgomery (Benched)* — defensemen for the Gold, giant nerd

*Angelica Shallows (Benched)* — engineer at RoboTech, also a giant nerd

*Blue Anderson (Breakaway)* — top forward in the league and for the Gold

*Anna Hayes (Breakaway)* — Max's former nanny, no relation to Kevin Hayes

*Rebecca Stravokraus (Breakout)* — Gold publicist, makes killer brownies, known at PR-Rebecca

*Kevin Hayes (Breakout)* — forward for the Gold, no relation to Anna Hayes

*Rebecca Hallbright (Checked)* — nutritionist for the Gold, plethora of delicious vegan recipes, known as Nutrionist-Rebecca

*Gabe Carter (Checked)* — doctor, head trainer for the Gold

*Calle Stevens (Coasting)* — assistant coach for the Gold, former national team member

*Coop Armstrong (Coasting)* — talented forward on the Gold, addicted to historical romance audiobooks

*Mia Caldwell (Centered)* — 5th degree black belt, brings the snark

*Liam Williamson (Centered)* — Gold forward finding his love for the game, charming and pushy in equal measures

*Charlotte Harris (Charging)* — new Gold GM, hates losing and the game Chubby Bunny

*Logan Walker (Charging)* — defensemen for the Gold, skills include: cockiness and being able to buy presents that make Charlotte squirm

*Devon Scott (Block & Tackle)* — former player, current owner Prestige Media group

*Becca Scott (Block & Tackle)* — Devon's assistant

**Additional Characters:**

*Bernard* — head coach

*Richie* — equipment manager

*Dan Plantain* — Brit's brother

*Diane Barie* — Stefan's mom

*Pierre Barie* — Stefan's dad, owner of the Gold

*Spence* — former goalie, married to Monique, daughter Mirabel

*Monique* — married to Spence, former model

*Mirabel* — daughter of Spence and Monique

*Mitch* — Sara's boss

*Allison and Sean* — Blane's parents

*Pascal* — Devon Scott's security lead

*Roger Shallows* — Mandy's dad

*Grant and Megan* — Devon's parents

# PROLOGUE

## NUTRITIONIST REBECCA

S he'd been trying to slip by the happy couple without ruining the romantic moment Kevin had planned for Bex. But they were right by the front door, and they'd see her if she moved forward.

And the guys were behind her, along with the girls.

All of whom were perfectly lovely people.

But she'd reached her limit on socializing for the day.

Thus her pinned-in position in the hall. She was desperate to be out of here, more than desperate to get back to her empty and quiet house, slip into her pajamas, and watch Hallmark movies through the night.

God, life was so much simpler in Hallmark movies.

Kevin jumped up and kissed Bex and when it seemed as though they were fully distracted, Rebecca made her move, slipping past them on quiet feet and opening the front door.

She'd just begun to close it quietly when a hand shot through the opening and prevented the door from shutting. Rebecca didn't scream because Kev and Bex were still only feet away, but she also didn't scream because her body already knew who it was. Her traitorous body, that was.

Gabe pushed through the opening and quietly closed the door behind him.

"You're leaving," he said.

Nope. Not doing this.

Ignoring him, Rebecca turned and started for her car. She'd purposely parked it where she wouldn't be blocked in.

Girl scout, she was. Always planning ahead.

Always running.

"Rebecca."

She kept walking.

She might work with Gabe, but she sure as heck wasn't on speaking terms with him. He'd dismissed her work, ignored her contribution to the team. He'd made her feel small and unimportant and—

She'd had too much of that in her life already.

So she kept walking.

"*Rebecca.*"

Not happening. Her car was in sight, thank fuck. She reached for the handle, glad her new car's locks opened automatically when the key fob was near.

He caught her arm.

"Baby—"

"I am *not* your baby, and you don't get to touch me." She ripped herself free, began muttering as she reached for the handle of her car again. "You don't even like me."

He stepped close, real close. Not touching her, not pushing the boundary she'd set, and yet he still got really freaking close. Her breath caught, her chin lifted, her pulse picked up. "That. Is. Where. You're. Wrong."

She froze.

"What?"

His mouth dropped to her ear, still not touching, but near enough that she could feel his hot breath.

"I like you, Rebecca. Too fucking much."

Then he turned and strode away.

# ONE

"So," she concluded, closing the slideshow presentation she'd been giving to the coaching and training staff of the Gold hockey team, "I'm suggesting that after the All-Star break, we start making the shift from animal proteins to plant. We would start small since we're in the middle of the season, just adding some smoothies and a few dishes in the team rooms, but if that goes well—and I think it'll give us a needed push going into playoff season—I'd propose a full shift for next season." She sucked in a breath. "My plan is solid, and athletes who follow similar diets are feeling better, playing harder, and more importantly, are less injury-prone—"

"That's a little grandiose."

Rebecca froze. "What?"

Gabe shifted in his seat, crossing one slack-covered leg over the other, leaning back to fold his arms over his chest. She had a hard time not letting her gaze linger approvingly on the powerful thighs, the gorgeous chest, and the arms those movements highlighted.

But then he spoke, and she found her focus.

Because as always, he was an asshole.

"The research on this is incomplete."

Well, not an asshole so much as never giving an inch, never failing to point out if there was the barest amount of exaggeration in her statements.

He was literal.

Didn't work in grandiosity.

But he only ever seemed to push back with her.

She'd have said it was because he had issues with women, that he was a classic case misogynist, but the Gold was the newest expansion team in the NHL and part of being the newest meant that they didn't abide by the good ole boy's club rules. There were lots of women on staff, nearly forty percent in most departments, and the administration had made a commitment to having gender equality in all groups in the next few years.

They had begun with Brit, the first female player in the league, then had hired Mandy as head trainer, and more recently had brought Calle Stevens on board as an assistant coach. The former national team player was supremely talented and had a unique style of play that lent itself to the Gold.

Then there was her. The second Rebecca, behind the very brash and equally brilliant Rebecca Stravokraus, the publicist for the team and PR guru. Second because she was quiet, because her job was less important . . . in some people's eyes.

Speaking of which, she narrowed hers at Gabe. "The research is promising, and many of the best athletes in other sports have made the switch to great success."

"Like who?"

She named some of the star athletes currently dominating the basketball courts and football fields.

"They are strong and explosive in their movements," she said. "Just like our players. They're less injury-prone, putting up big numbers. But you're right," she admitted, "this isn't a magic solution. No diet plan will be."

"So, your research is anecdotal at best."

"N-no," she said and sucked in a breath. "If you'd look at the index—"

Gabe wasn't listening. He huffed out a laugh. "The guys work hard. They need protein and not just froufrou hippie—"

Bernard, the head coach of the team, stood. "I'll let you two argue it out." He glanced at his watch. "Keep me posted on what you decide. For now, I have another meeting."

Rebecca's hands were shaking with fury, but she forced herself to meet his gaze and nodded. A moment later, he'd gathered his belongings and left, the rest of the room's occupants beginning to follow suit.

None of them could know how much it had cost her to ask for the meeting, to stand up there and present her idea to them.

Gentle fingers on her arm.

Rebecca glanced up and saw that Mandy was standing in front of her, softness in her expression. "I'll talk to him."

She shook her head. "No—"

The softness in her friend's face faded. "He's being an ass."

It didn't take a rocket scientist to know the *he* Mandy was referring to.

Yes, Gabe was. But—

"He's not necessarily wrong," she began. "The research is—"

"Gabe gets tunnel vision," Mandy said. "I mean, I love the man and he's one of my oldest friends, but the biggest strike against him as a doctor is his inability to think outside of his original paradigm. He gets onto a path and forgets to consider all the outside possibilities, even the ones he might have discounted initially as outliers."

Rebecca grasped on to that knowledge with both hands, tucking the snippet close, knowing it would be helpful in dealing with Gabe in the future.

But it didn't take away the sting now.

"It's fine," she said, tucking her laptop into her backpack. "I'll keep monitoring the research and present again at the beginning of next season."

Ten more months to prepare herself for another firing squad.

"I don't think we should drop—"

"I'm sorry to interrupt, but . . ."

A voice that was almost musical, sweet and lovely and totally unmatched with the type of player Calle Stevens had been on the ice—which was dominating, intense, and physical.

"You're not interrupting, Calle," Mandy said, always pleasant, always so at ease in social situations. "We were just discussing how much of a pain in the ass our Dr. Gabe Carter can be." She raised her voice on the last, loud enough that Gabe heard it from where he'd paused by the door.

He mock-glared. "Thorough isn't a pain in the ass."

"It is if you're *ignoring the obvious*!" Mandy sing-songed back.

Calle snorted.

Gabe shook his head and strode out of the room.

Mandy turned back to face them.

Rebecca sucked in a breath to steady her voice and forced her eyes to meet Mandy's then Calle's. That was the worst part, the eye contact. Not knowing what her face betrayed, if they could see how much of a mess she was underneath.

Calle's lips were curved. "Gabe is . . . interesting."

Mandy huffed. "Interesting is one word for him," she muttered then smiled widely, explaining to Calle, "I can only freely grumble because I've known the PIA for more than a decade."

"Ah." Calle held up the papers Rebecca had passed out during the meeting. "Well, I don't want to stop you guys from doing . . . *that*, but I did have a few more questions about the diet you were proposing."

"O-oh, I-I," Rebecca stammered, clenching the straps on her backpack like it was her lifeline. "I—"

Calle touched her shoulder. "Can we grab a coffee tomorrow?" Rebecca bit her lip. One on one with a person she was just coming to know? That was almost as bad as giving the presentation in the first place. "I would stay today, but I have to get to that same meeting as Bernard. I do want to learn more, even if you don't have time tomorrow."

"I—uh . . ."

"I have a few more questions too, so why don't we all meet for tea?" Mandy suggested, and Rebecca's chest relaxed as her friend saved her. "Ten-thirty at Molly's?"

Calle nodded. "Works for me."

Mandy smiled, bumped Rebecca's shoulder. "I'll see you tomorrow," she said. "I've got to get to the training suite then home."

"Will you walk with me on your way?" Calle asked. "I've got a couple of questions for you too."

"Sure," Mandy said, moving with Calle to the door. "What did you need . . .?"

Their voices trailed off as they walked out of the room and down the hall.

Rebecca was alone.

She released a long, slow breath, crossed to the door, and flicked off the lights. But she didn't go out, just leaned back against the piece of wood, backpack clutched in her arms, and breathed.

She was alone.

That was right.

That was best.

That was all she could ask for.

# Two

S he spent longer than she cared to admit leaning against that wall, coaxing herself into moving, into leaving that room.

But eventually she managed.

The halls were quiet, mostly empty of players, off for the Christmas holiday—many were hanging out with family in the Bay Area, but others had gone home to Canada or Europe or returned to families in different parts of the U.S. It was pretty much staff-only at the rink this week of the year, everything winding down in many ways, while prep for the push of the second half of the season was already beginning to ramp up.

Hence her proposal on a diet.

Sighing, she made a quick stop at her office to grab her purse then stepped back out into the hall, smiling as she hurried past a harried-but-pleased-looking Bex. Probably because of the huge teddy bear that had been taking up a good portion of her office.

So much of the space that Bex hadn't been able to close the door.

But Kevin, her boyfriend and a player on the Gold, was absolutely perfect for the publicist, just the right amount of pushy and sweet to get through the armor around Bex's heart. He'd needed to be pushy, too. That armor had been thick as hell. But they were happy now, and Rebecca knew they'd go the distance.

She had a sixth sense about relationships.

Just not the courage to go for one of her own.

Her mind was stuck on the giant fuzzy pink bear, gripping a huge heart that had been emblazoned with *I'll Always Love You For Your Brownies*—an ode to the killer dessert Bex made, so good that even Rebecca gave up her no refined sugar, no bleached flour diet to have a taste when they were around—and so she missed the man blocking her way to the exit.

She was *always* aware of her exits. *Always.*

Except this time.

And it was going to cost her.

"Whoa there."

Warm hands on her arms, a big body too close—

"Rebecca—"

"Sorry," she said, jumping back, eyes on the floor. She clutched her purse tighter, shifting to the side so she could shuffle past Gabe and escape, pretending he was just another normal human of the world and not a man that made her typically tripping heart skip double-time.

He didn't move, just let their bodies brush against each other as she slid by. Her cheeks went hot, a shiver skated down her spine, but as much as her body seemed to scream her attraction to Gabe, her mind was stronger. That contact was too intense. Filled with too many sensations.

He was unsafe.

So *freaking* dangerous.

A hand on her shoulder. Heat exploded on her skin from that simple contact of his palm, spreading, flaring out through her body until it wasn't just her cheeks that felt hot, but also every single nerve. She needed—

"Rebecca—"

*Run*, her mind screamed.

*Stay*, her body countered. *Get closer.*

That conflict, the equal and opposing forces, had the handcuffs that normally tied down her tongue unlocking, dropping to the ground, keeping her rooted in place when otherwise she might have run. But then again, many of the anxieties that made it so difficult for her to interact with people seemed to disappear when she was with Gabe.

Case in point, the words and tone that came out of her mouth in that moment.

"You're an asshole," she snapped, whipping around to face him. "You know that, right?"

His head jerked back, her outburst almost a physical slap. "What?"

Despite the lack of anxiety with Gabe, she still had never spoken to him that way. Yes, she was typically very quiet. Yes, that sometimes came off as bitchy.

No, that didn't mean she was anything but professional when it came to her interactions with the team, players, *or* staff. If anything, she was cold and rigid, or at least that was how she'd heard Gabe describe her to Mandy.

*She's so stiff, I don't think it's a stick up her ass, it's an icicle,* he'd told Mandy one day in the training suite, obviously not realizing that Rebecca had been passing by them in the hall. *Rebecca needs to get away from her granola recipes and find a life.*

Ouch.

There was a reason she avoided open doors and conversations taking place within them. It didn't feel great to eavesdrop, especially on unpleasant musings about her and her asshole.

And she didn't mean Gabe.

He wouldn't be *her* anything. Not ever.

She lifted her chin, yanked her shoulder free of his grip. "You're a jerk," she said, the burst of anger already fading, the urge to get small again seeping forward. But she managed to keep her voice from shaking. "You—"

"You're right."

She'd been frantically searching her mind for the right words, but his stopped her.

"I should have listened first." He held up a stack of papers, and she recognized the top one as a study she'd cited in her presentation. "I printed these off. I spent the last hour reading up on this and—"

"*You* read up?"

He stopped. "Yeah—"

"You. *Read*. Up."

The anger was back.

His brows knit together, drawing her attention to rich brown eyes. Her breath caught at the color, and she realized for all the fleeting contact she'd allowed herself with his gaze, she'd never stared long enough to recognize the depth of colors in his irises.

It reminded her of quinoa, pale brown laced with deep mahogany.

Pretty.

But then he smirked. And spoke.

Pretty disappeared.

"I'm a doctor, Rebecca," he said drolly. "I do know how to read."

Fury took its place.

"And perhaps did you read any of those papers I passed out during the presentation?" she asked with clenched teeth.

His lips pressed flat. "No," he said. "I prefer to do my own research—"

"Asshole," she growled and snatched the papers from his hands. "Did you realize that your *research* mirrored mine? Or that I gave you *this* study"—she held it up, flipped to the next—"and *this* one. Oh! And *this* one, too." She shoved the stack of papers back at him. "So, please mansplain to me some more about your *research*."

"I—" He broke off, gaze locking with hers.

And it was too much. Her eyes dropped to the floor, chest

heaving, fire fading. "Whatever, Gabe. Keeping researching, keep proving to yourself that you're the smartest and know the most and your way is always the best—"

"I just said you were right."

"After you belittled me in front of the rest of the team."

"I asked questions."

"No, you discounted my idea without taking time to understand the thought and research that went into my proposal," she said, volume dropping, words beginning to shake. "You could have said, *I have concerns, let's look into this further.* Or hell, perhaps, *I'll read the sources that you provided, do some further research, and then we can make a decision.*" She released a shuddering breath. "I have a doctorate in nutrition. This is my passion, my life-blood, and you . . . didn't care. And now you're coming to me with so-called sources proclaiming it a good idea. Sorry, but th-that's—"

"A dick move," he finished when she faltered.

She nodded. "Yes." A beat as she waited for him to continue talking to say anything else.

But he didn't.

And so she pushed past him and hurried from the building. To her car. To her apartment.

Where it was quiet. Where she was alone.

Where it was safe.

---

Her sister called that evening, but Rebecca didn't muster the courage to pick up the phone. Between the presentation and the confrontation with Gabe, not to mention the impending tea date with Calle and Mandy, she was an absolute disaster.

And if there was one thing her sister had little patience for, it was Rebecca being an absolute disaster.

Eighteen years older than her, Sandra had been the mother neither of them had experienced. Responsible, detail-oriented, an absolute rule-follower. But she hadn't been particularly soft or caring or empathetic, especially when Rebecca began showing similar characteristics to their flighty, negligent mother.

What Sandra could never seem to understand was that while Rebecca might have anxiety, might have a similar personality to their mom, she also had pieces that Sandra had given her. Perseverance, integrity, an incredible work ethic.

So while the anxiety she battled was sometimes crippling, Rebecca always pushed through to the other side.

She'd gotten her doctorate, was working in a position that challenged and enlightened her on a daily basis, and she'd even recently accepted an offer to release a series of books based on the lifestyle blog she'd started nearly a decade before. That blog was her secret outlet, a safe place she could be herself because the real world was scary.

No one knew about the blog.

Well, no one she talked to on a regular basis, that was. Which meant that Sandra didn't know and neither did her coworkers.

Being a registered dietician meant that she'd worked in different capacities over the years, first while she'd been getting her masters and PhD, then before she'd found a full-time position with athletes, as was her dream. Initially, she'd worked at hospitals and nursing homes, then with colleges and minor league teams, and finally she'd gotten her position with the Gold.

Now she was in her mid-thirties, working her dream job, and . . . dealing with men like Gabe.

Not fair. But also . . .

Yes, her feelings had been hurt.

Yes, she was still going to go to work tomorrow.

She'd do what she did best, pretend and move on.

But for *that* night, she ignored her sister's call, took a long ass bath, then slipped into her rattiest sweats and coziest sweatshirt. She'd huddle, recover, get stronger. And tomorrow she would have tea with Calle and Mandy.

She'd talk about the diet plan. She'd answer questions and share insights.

She'd interact, no matter how challenging.

But that would happen *tomorrow*.

Tonight she would soak in the tub alone, exactly like she preferred.

Even if she spent a lot of that alone time wondering if it was actually being by herself that she had a preference for, or if it was because being alone was all she knew.

———

Molly's was one of those rare places she could count on.

Fresh, fabulous food, plenty of tables—including ones safely tucked into corners—and low-pressure ordering.

They never looked at her with impatience if she stuttered or changed her mind, and with the cozy seat cushions, sleek granite tabletops on tables that never wobbled, and lots of vegan options, it was her go-to.

They also served her favorite organic pomegranate green tea.

Or they had begun carrying it after Rebecca had haltingly mentioned it as her preferred variety one time in passing to the owner, Molly.

Reason number 642 why Molly's was great.

The waiter, Tom, brought her tea almost before she sat her butt down at the table—okay, it was almost like *her* table because she was in so often. "Salad today, Rebecca?" he asked.

"Not today."

With a nod, he left her to it and she spent the next few minutes booting up her laptop and opening the presentation on the screen, along with the research she'd gathered.

"Whew!" Calle said, sinking into the chair opposite her with a flurry of movements. "I'll never get used to how the weather changes in this city. I was frozen an hour ago and now I'm sweating."

"And welcome to winter in San Francisco," Mandy said, walking in behind her and sitting with much less fluster. She picked up a menu from the holder on the table. "You *have* to try their salads, Calle."

Calle made a face. "I've decided I'm adult enough to avoid eating my veggies."

Rebecca gasped.

Mandy laughed.

Calle smiled. "I'm kidding, of course." A shrug. "Sort of. How about I'll consume a reasonable amount for my status as an adult?"

Rebecca glanced down at her hands, feeling a little like an idiot for not having realized that Calle was joking. "T-that sounds good," she said softly then forced her eyes back up. "Should we talk about how we're going to force the guys to eat them instead?"

Mandy grinned. "Definitely. I can't wait to torture Blane."

"I'm not sure that's how relationships are supposed to work," Calle said, lips twitching as she reached for a menu. "Are you eating?"

"I—" She'd been planning on not, on having an escape route so she wasn't tied down with a plate of food, but dammit this was Molly's and she wanted one of their salads.

"Of course, she is," Mandy said, answering for her as Tom came back over to take the rest of the drink orders.

"The girls changed my mind," she said when he glanced down at her.

"Good," he replied. "Molly just pulled the candied nuts out of the oven." He winked and Mandy snorted, which made Rebecca relax enough to giggle. Calle, much more open with her feelings, laughed outright.

"That's what all the boys say," she quipped.

Which made Rebecca giggle again and Mandy demand, "More candied nuts!"

Tom disappeared with a salute and they continued talking, drifting into discussing the nutrition plan.

"Will it be personalized for each player?" Calle asked.

"For sure," she said, pouring more tea into her cup. "Some of the needs are similar, but allergies and food sensitivities have to be considered, along with where we are in the season or if they need a boost to help them recover from an injury."

"I wish I had you when I blew out my knee," Calle said. "I tried to come back afterward, but no amount of rehab could get it to where it once was." She sighed. "Not that I don't like coaching and don't feel incredibly lucky to have this job as well as having gone out after playing on that gold medal team, but . . ."

"It's not the same standing on the sidelines as being in the game."

Mandy and Calle both looked up at her in shock.

Rebecca shrugged. "Or I'd guess th-that was—"

Mandy reached across the table, squeezed her hand.

"That's exactly how it is," Calle said.

"But you push through and find other ways to find your happy," Mandy told them. "You pivot and transform and . . . you summon up the courage to grab on to it when the opportunity comes along."

She and Calle glanced at Mandy.

"Whoa," Calle eventually said. "That was deep."

Mandy snorted, opened her mouth, but was interrupted by Tom dropping off their plates of food. "Get deep on those nuts," she quipped, picking up her fork.

"*Oooh,*" Calle said on a laugh. "I like this side of you."

"What? The unprofessional one?"

"Yes. That, exactly."

Rebecca laughed as they continued bantering, starting in on her salad, and while she shook her head, it was with a smile on her face because she was having a good time.

Socializing.

Who knew that was even possible?

———

Over the next few days, she managed to socialize a bit more, or at least to finalize her plan with Calle and Mandy over another lunch at Molly's and then reintroduce it to Gabe and the rest of the training staff.

They were giving her initial roll-out a trial period after the break.

Then they would reevaluate.

But Rebecca felt like she'd been filled with helium, she was so buoyant and excited they were giving her plan a chance. If it worked out, it would mean a ton more leg work for her going into next season, but she was thrilled to be given the opportunity and was going to make sure absolutely every detail was hammered out before the players returned for training camp.

This was new and exciting and because it was food and diet plans and nutrition, instead of being panicked at the thought of all the work ahead of her, she was excited.

Just think of all the office supplies she got to buy.

Blue Post-Its, green ones. Hell, maybe she'd even splurge for pink. And file folders, do *not* get her started on file folders.

She snorted and obeyed her phone when it ordered her to make a left turn. There was a reason she was thinking about food and nutrition, and that was because she was forcing herself to undergo even more socializing that evening.

Christmas Gold-style.

Just the thought of being around that many people was terrifying, but she was doing it anyway.

Look at her go. Socialization multiple times in one week.

Go her.

She made the final turn and saw the line of cars parked along the street and in the driveway, carefully picking a spot that made sure she wouldn't be blocked in. Then she turned off her car and breathed.

"I can do this," she commanded, though her heart was pounding. "You know all these people. It will be fine."

Bathroom. She needed to find out where that was first thing. And scope out the food. And—

A knock at her window had her jumping.

"Hey!" Mandy called through the glass.

Both more nerves and less. She had to go now, couldn't put her car back into drive and leave. But she'd also have a friend. Sucking in a breath and straightening her shoulders, she reached for her purse. "You can do this."

Mandy stepped back when Rebecca opened the door. Blane walked up to join them, their baby girl, Madeline, in his arms. "I'm so ready for pie," he declared, tossing Madeline high enough that Rebecca gasped.

Mandy just smiled, especially when Madeline giggled.

"Come on," Mandy said. "Less tossing of the baby. I thought you'd give your mother a heart attack last time she saw you do that."

Blane grinned. "Maddy loves it," he said, nuzzling their daughter. "Don't you, baby girl?"

Rebecca relaxed, reaching into the backseat of her car for the brussels sprout dish she'd brought.

Mandy snagged Madeline, Blane stole the bag she was carrying then turned to Rebecca and also took the dish from her hands—

"Oh," she exclaimed. "You don't have—"

But he was already walking to the house.

"I know I don't have to," he called over his shoulder. "Hurry up, before all the pie is gone!"

"With all the rookies around," Mandy said, "he might be in for a rude awakening for what food might have survived the ride . . . or the first five minutes, anyway."

"They do seem to consume an insane amount of food."

Mandy flashed her a smile, untangling Madeline's hand from her hair. "I heard Kevin bought a ring."

"Me, too," Rebecca murmured. Part of the reason she'd come when Kevin had asked. Her friends deserved to share their happiness with people, even if one of these people happened to be an awkward, anxious woman with more baggage than an airport.

She could suck it up and find a way to put that aside for a few hours.

Mandy nodded, lips twitching. "Speaking of rude awakenings," she said. "Bex is going to freak."

"She sure is," Rebecca agreed.

She walked up the path and into the house, Mandy at her side, completely oblivious to the fact that the *she* was the Rebecca about to have a rude awakening.

If she'd known the next few hours were going to change her life, then there was no way she *ever* would have agreed to come.

In the end, she wasn't sure if that rude awakening had been good.

Or bad. Really, really bad.

# THREE

GABE

He watched Rebecca slip from the house, head down, shoulders bowed in on themselves, and his feet were moving almost before he consciously knew he was following her.

Red hair trailing in waves down her back.

Tall and slender—she took her nutrition ideas to heart—but no diet plan could take away that fabulous ass.

Two perfect handfuls of woman he wanted to grab hold of.

And he'd fucked up any chance of that by being a dick.

Probably safer that way for her. He wasn't in the market for a relationship, not after his ex had destroyed him.

Being tied to a woman was way too complicated.

But he still followed Rebecca out, sticking a hand into the opening of the door just before it closed. He halted its progress, slipped out.

"You're leaving," he said.

She froze, green eyes wide on his. Fuck, she was pretty.

With a huff, she spun away and began walking toward her car parked near the edge of the property.

"Rebecca," he called, following her.

She kept walking.

Fucking hell, he didn't like that. Not when—

*What, asshole?* his conscience chimed in. *You don't want her, so just leave her alone.*

Except, he *did* want her. Mostly because she was beautiful and smart and when he could get her to say a few words, she was funny. But part of him also wanted her because she reminded him of—

Not. Going. There.

"Rebecca."

She reached for the driver's side door handle.

He caught her arm. "Baby—"

"I am *not* your baby," she snapped, "and *you* don't get to touch me." She yanked her arm with more strength than he'd expected, considering her waif-like body, and pulled free, reaching for the handle of her car again. "You don't even like me."

He stepped close, real close. Not touching her when she'd told him not to, but still close enough to get a whiff of cinnamon.

Cinnamon. He inhaled deeply. Fucking spice.

Fucking *hell.*

"That. Is. Where. You're. Wrong."

Her jaw dropped open. "What?"

He bent his head, spoke directly into her ear, a soft floral scent mixing with all that cinnamon, making his head spin, and him blurt.

"I like you, Rebecca. Too fucking much."

Then he turned and strode back to the house, listening to the slam of her car door, the rev of the engine as he did an admirable job of scaring her away.

# FOUR

## REBECCA

S he was avoiding going into work.

It was Monday morning. It was after Christmas. It was . . . two days since Gabe had cornered her outside her car and had declared—

*I like you, Rebecca. Too fucking much.*

And all weekend long, those words had been cycling through her mind like a mini tornado.

*I like you. Too fucking much. I like you. Too—*

Which made absolutely no sense. Gabe didn't like her. She was too rigid, had too big of an icicle up her ass. Plus, *she* didn't like him. He was arrogant and narrow-minded and—

She sighed and slipped on her flats.

He was not going to be the reason she failed at her job.

She'd gotten phase one of the diet plan approved.

Several of the players were coming in that day to discuss it and the accommodations she'd make for allergies. Then before next season, Rebecca would be in individual meetings with each of them—those in permanent positions as well as those who'd be participating in training camp and didn't have a roster spot yet.

Regardless, the idea was to get everyone on board with the diet and to adjust it for any necessary allergies, sensitivities, food preferences, or other accommodations such as requests to keep in lean proteins like fish and the occasional chicken. or some like Max's—one of their star defensemen's—request for a weekly cheat day. He'd found out about the plan at the party, along with her thoughts on how she wanted to expand it for next season and made the appeal, which she thought was fair.

Once next year's schedule was released, and if it was approved, Rebecca would just have to come up with a plan for that, as well as a schedule of times that would be best to take a break from the diet. She planned on looking at the games and anticipated practices, knowing that any cheat days shouldn't come on those, while also knowing that the diet was going to be restrictive for many of the players and they needed to be satisfied enough that they would actually be willing to try *and* stick with it.

She could only control the food the guys had access to at the Gold facilities and any team meals that were provided. Other than that, the players ate on their own, and she knew for her plan to be successful, they'd need to be committed.

Hence, all the interactions she was forcing on herself that day. She needed to address any concerns and accommodations for phase one to go well so they could move on to phase two.

She hoped it would, because it would be good for her, job experience-wise, and great for the team.

Or at least that was what she was telling herself.

"Stop stalling," she muttered and slipped her purse onto her shoulder then forced her feet to move to the door. "This is what you wanted, what you believed in."

Right.

There was that.

And so, she walked downstairs to her car, got in, and didn't allow herself any extra time before pulling out of the lot and onto the road that led to the rink. Neither did she delay in the parking lot, or walking down the hall to her office.

She didn't even hesitate in answering the knock on her door that signaled her first appointment.

Something funny happened.

Without allowing those stalls, those excuses, those postpone-ments, the day kept right on moving. The minutes passed, along with the hours. And the meetings were . . . tolerable?

Perhaps not the most ringing endorsement ever, but they weren't as horrible as she'd imagined. In fact, the ones with Max and Brit were almost enjoyable.

She'd even sort of forgotten that she was purposefully avoiding Gabe.

See? Win-win all around.

Snorting, she flicked off the light for her office and stepped into the hall, thinking about how good the meal she'd thrown in the Crock-Pot that morning would make her apartment smell when she walked through the door. Peppers, onions, and garlic made anything taste good, but most especially the mix of wild rice and tofu she'd left simmering that morning.

Her mouth watered and she picked up her pace, closing the door behind her and walking down the hall to her car. It was late, so the space was mostly empty, and the few interactions she had were limited to simple waves or 'Hellos.'

Probably a good thing since she was maxing out on social for the day.

The first sign of trouble was the fact that her car door didn't automatically unlock when she tugged on the driver's side handle, but she didn't immediately process that fact because the car was new and she was still getting used to all the fancy bells and whis-tles, including doors that unlocked when she approached the vehicle rather than having to use her key fob.

The second was the complete lack of power when she pressed the button to start her hybrid.

The third—

Well, who was she kidding? There was no third. That is, unless someone counted banging her head against the steering wheel as trouble. Which it probably was . . . but regardless, she was sitting in her car, her forehead against the fabric-wrapped wheel when the knock came on her window.

She jumped, head whipping around to see Gabe peering in at her.

It was winter in northern California, which meant that at nearly nine, the sky was pitch black, but she always parked under an exterior light and so she could see Gabe quiet clearly.

And there was a lot of him to see.

So much more than the previous week. So much more than before he'd said he'd liked her.

She'd obviously acknowledged he was handsome somewhere on her mental registry. That was an indisputable fact. But it had also been easy to compartmentalize that away because she'd known Gabe wasn't for her. Thus, any attraction had been shoved *way* down.

That had been before *I like you.*

Three words she'd never heard from a man before. Three *terrifying* words. And yet, three words that had flayed her to her core because they'd cracked open that door she'd thrown up between herself and the possibility of any type of normal relationship.

She had anxiety.

Her mother also had it.

Rebecca had seen what it had done to her parents' marriage, how it had crippled her mother, infuriated her father, taken so many choices away from her sister. Even though Rebecca had gotten help for the worst of her anxiety, many days were still a struggle, and she'd promised herself when she'd begun therapy almost ten years before that she wouldn't be a burden on her partner, wouldn't have kids and burden them—either by making them step up and act like a parent—as her sister had been forced to do—or to pass on this illness that made what most thought of as simple everyday tasks seem almost insurmountable.

Avoiding the connection of a partner was smarter. And it was safer for everyone involved. Easier—

Another knock had her blinking and cracking open the door.

"You okay?" Gabe asked.

"I-I'm fine," she said and closed it.

He opened it back up. "Rebecca. You—"

She yanked on the handle, almost succeeded in shutting it again, but before it latched, Gabe had tugged it wide enough to fit his hips in the gap, which put a certain part of his anatomy right in her face.

She slammed her palms over her eyes.

Which gave him time and opportunity to push the door all the way open and then crouch down in front of her and peel her fingers back.

"Hey."

Her breath caught. She shook her head.

"Rebecca. Are you okay?"

A nod. "I'm fine. My car isn't."

He frowned then reached over and pressed the button on the far side of the steering wheel. Predictably, nothing happened.

Irritated, she slapped his hand away. "Back up. My car won't start. I'll call Triple A."

Though she was in a safe spot, this *was* San Francisco and so, it would take a long time for a tow truck to make its way to her. She stifled a sigh, knowing the wait she had in front of her was going to feel interminable, especially when she was already exhausted after the meetings and social interactions of the day.

Gabe seemed to recognize that because he reached across her and unclicked her seat belt, snagging her purse from the passenger's seat as she was still processing his initial movements.

Then her hand was in his and he was tugging her out of the car.

"Come on," he said, "I'll give you a ride. You can deal with this in the morning."

She might as well have turned into a bobble-head for the

amount of shaking her noggin was doing that evening. "I can't just leave it—"

"I'll call security on the way, make sure they know." He pulled her keys from her purse and locked the door then took off in the direction of his car.

*What the hell was happening here?*

Rebecca stared after him for nearly a minute before pulling herself together and trailing after him. When she neared the midsized SUV, he crossed around the hood and sat down in the driver's seat, leaving her with very little choice but to open the door in front of her and sit in the passenger's seat.

"You know," she muttered. "I can just go inside and catch a ride from Bex."

"Kevin packed her off an hour ago." He started up the car and backed out of the spot.

"Mandy—"

"Gone."

"Brit—"

"Departed."

She paused then snapped, "What? Are you trying to go through every option in the thesaurus entry for *left*?"

A flash of white teeth. "If I did, I forgot some good ones. Absconded." He tapped his chin. "Or vamoosed, for example."

"I can't believe you." She clenched her jaw tightly, gritting out, "You are absolutely *unbelievable*."

"And *I* like that I'm the only one who gets to see this side of you."

Her lips clamped together, throat going dry.

"Everyone else gets the quiet, reserved Rebecca, and I get"— he glanced at her—"fire."

Fire.

*Fire?*

That made absolutely no sense. She wasn't fire. She was cold. She was closed down. She—

"I thought I had an icicle up my ass," she blurted.

They slid to a stop when the signal in front of them turned red, and that ill timing meant Gabe had the opportunity to glance over at her and the occasion to study her closely.

Or at least her profile.

Because she sure as shit wasn't going to look at him.

"I've been an asshole," he admitted. "For a long time. I—" He shook his head. "It doesn't matter, really. But I let personal stuff bleed into work, and you did nothing more than have the bad luck to—"

A horn blared, making them both jump.

Gabe hit the accelerator but didn't continue talking, and as silence descended in the car, Rebecca couldn't stop herself from asking, "Bad luck to what?"

Silence for long enough that she didn't think he'd answer. "To remind me of my ex."

"I remind you of your ex?"

"Too much."

Oh.

*Oh.*

Well that was—

"She—" He sighed. "That's not fair. She might have the same look as you. Pretty green eyes, olive skin, red hair. But that's not what makes you two alike."

The tone of his voice made it virtually impossible for her to figure out if that was a good or bad thing. She would have immediately assumed that it was a bad thing, based on the negative connotation of *ex*, but there was something in Gabe's tone— longing maybe, melancholy definitely.

"I fucked up with her, and seeing you every day was like a slap in the face."

Rebecca was quiet for a long moment. "At first, I thought we were having this conversation for you to apologize for being a jerk, or maybe for you to clue me in to your behavior so we could make amends."

A beat. "That *is* what I'm trying to do."

"Well, you're failing at it."

"I—"

"You see me, and I'm a slap in the face. Your behavior has been skewed by your ex, but that doesn't excuse it. You were unprofessional, and I suffered because of it." She sucked in a breath. "Does that about cover it?"

Gabe pulled the car over to the side of the road. "I'm fucking this up, aren't I?"

She rolled her eyes. "What gave it away?"

"I'm trying to apologize—"

"How about you start with the two words *I'm* and *sorry*?"

His lips twitched. "I'm sorry."

"Great."

The twitch turned into a curve of his mouth. "Good."

"Now, we can move on."

An expression crossed his face, but before she could process what it meant, he glanced behind him to check traffic and pulled back onto the road. A few blocks later, he finally agreed, "Now we can move on."

But something about his tone struck her as wrong.

Before she could work up the courage to find out why, he asked her for her address, which was really something he should have done before leaving the lot, but she decided this wasn't the moment to bring that up. Instead, she rattled it off and didn't add anything further to the conversation aside from a simple, "left here," "take this exit," and an "up ahead on the right."

Fifteen quiet minutes later, he'd pulled into her parking spot in front of her apartment complex, and threw the SUV in park, then made his way around to open the passenger door before she'd unbuckled her seat belt.

She put out her hand for her purse.

Gabe didn't pass it over, but his voice was gentle. "I'll walk you up."

Rebecca waggled her fingers. "I'm fine."

"I'll walk you up." The gentle disappeared, granite appearing in its place, and she mentally weighed her options for a heartbeat before deciding that giving in would get her to her apartment sooner, and that meant wild rice and garlic and comfy sweatpants would quickly follow.

She sighed. "Fine."

Then started for the stairs.

Gabe trailed her, and one flight later, they were outside her apartment.

"This is me," she said, holding out a hand for her purse.

He fished out her keys then handed them to her. Not what she wanted, but since it put her one step closer to sweatpants, she accepted them, unlocking the door and pushing it open. The delicious aroma of her simmering Crock-Pot greeted her, and she immediately inhaled deeply, pulling it further into her lungs. Then she shook herself and put her hand out for her purse again.

Gabe set it in her palm. "That smells delicious."

She smiled. "It *tastes* delicious."

He put his hands over his heart as though she had stabbed him. "That's just cruel."

Her heart skipped a beat as their eyes locked, and both of their mouths curved into grins, the moment stretching and tightening with a tension that was equally uncomfortable and intoxicating.

It was terrifying.

It was exhilarating.

It was unlike anything she'd ever experienced.

She nibbled at the corner of her mouth. He leaned closer—

Then took two steps back. "I'll see you tomorrow, Rebecca." Another retreating step. "You should lock up."

She didn't know what motivated her to say it, what force rose out of the awkward and anxious to extend the words. But then again, with Gabe, those nerves always seemed to fade away, and so perhaps the offer wasn't so surprising.

"Want to come in and try some?"

# FIVE

S o lovely and sweet.

So not for him.

Her cheeks flooded with pink as she invited him into her apartment. *Him*. The asshole who'd been on edge around her since she'd joined the team, who'd done his damnedest to ignore the fact that she was beautiful and reminded him far too much of his ex.

An ex he hadn't wanted to be an ex.

But who'd become one anyway.

Which was the exact reason he should turn around and leave Rebecca to her life, to commit to the plan he'd concocted— namely cooling his asshole-ness and keeping their relationship cordial and professional.

As he was thinking that, as the heartbeat of silence stretched longer, he watched the smile from her lips flatten out, the light in her expression disappear.

And he found that he couldn't allow that to happen, couldn't watch her turn into a diminished version of herself, not when he was the cause, not *ever*. So, he closed the distance between them, slipped past her and into her apartment, and declared, "You cooked, so I'm on dish duty."

Then he couldn't decide if that was the smartest or the stupidest thing he'd ever done.

In the end, it was both.

But in that moment, he couldn't have done anything else.

After a few seconds, Rebecca moved, flipping the lock on the door and setting her purse on a table that sat just inside the hall. Her gaze flitted to his then away and he kept watching, studying her as she straightened her shoulders and sucked in a breath.

Then she slipped off her shoes, tucked them neatly on the shoe rack that was placed next to the table, and moved toward him.

Cinnamon.

She always had the barest hint of spice wafting around her, but he hadn't been able to pinpoint where it came from. She didn't chew gum or pop mints. He'd never seen her put on lip balm or lotion.

So, was it just Rebecca?

Was she really spice, just hidden beneath shy?

Gabe had been trying to resist the urge to discover that for close to four years now.

And now he was in her apartment.

Brilliant move.

Because the scent of cinnamon was more intense inside her place, weaving together with the smell of whatever she had cooking. It soaked into his senses, drew him toward her.

She sidestepped him and moved into the open kitchen that took up one corner of the space, pulling out a drawer and rummaging around inside it for utensils. The pale gray drawers had feather-shaped handles, the cabinet doors circular crystal knobs that twinkled in the light.

Feather-shaped.

Twinkling crystals.

Now *that* was unexpected.

Turning, he studied the rest of her space. It wasn't cluttered in the least, and he would have been shocked to find it *wasn't* totally organized based on what he knew about her very deliberate and particular work habits, but he also hadn't expected so much . . . personality.

God, he was such an asshole.

Because he'd judged, he'd put her in the same category as Maggie, and perhaps worst—though probably not unexpected—considering that Mandy regularly told him he walked through life with blinders on, he'd taken the shield Rebecca presented to the world as if that was all she was.

And he'd missed out on the layers underneath.

He'd missed the sparkling crystal.

He'd missed that the hint of spice marked something truly special.

So, asshole.

"Crap," she gasped, causing him to jerk his gaze away from a floral couch that was really cool and somehow not girly, from the pretty tapestry of reds and purples that was draped over a window, from the complete and utter lack of clutter anywhere.

She set a bowl on the counter with a *clank* and hurried to the sink, turning on the water and shoving her hand underneath the stream.

He moved, closing the space between them and reaching down to grip her fingers in his. "Burn?"

A nod. "I-it's fine."

Gabe's eyes traced over the injured digit, identifying the reddened patch of skin that, while it probably stung, was as she said, fine. But he didn't want to let go of her hand just yet.

"What happened?"

She shook her head, that tiny little jerk of her head that was quintessentially Rebecca. "Nothing. Just splattered myself. It's stupid."

He shut off the water and carefully dried her hand, bringing it up to his mouth to press an unthinking kiss to the red mark. "I'm sorry you hurt yourself."

Her breath shuddered. "I'm fine."

His lips twitched as he gently lowered her hand and leaned around her to survey the countertop. She had the lid off the Crock-Pot, a ladle abandoned inside it, two bowls and spoons placed next to it. Nudging her over a few inches, he filled both bowls, snagged the spoons, and brought them to the table.

Then he picked up Rebecca's unhurt hand and tugged her out of the kitchen. "Sit. What do you want to drink?"

"Wine."

"You drink wine?"

"It's organic."

Gabe smirked. "Of course, it is."

She glared.

He laughed. "I'm teasing."

"You're not," she muttered. "But if you're not a jerk about it, I'll let you have a glass."

Hands rising in surrender, he said, "I'll be on my best behavior."

"Sure, you will," she grumbled but told him where the glasses and bottle, along with the opener, were. A few moments later, he was sitting down next to her at the worn oak table. It was different than the rest of her furniture, but it somehow fit. Probably because there was a collection of doilies—yes, fucking *doilies*—at the center, along with an incense holder. He touched a finger to the small pile of ash on the wood, brought it to his nose.

So *that* was what the cinnamon was from.

Rebecca studied him for a moment before glancing back down at her bowl and spooning up a bite.

He rubbed the ash between his finger and thumb, watching the gray coat his skin as the cinnamon scent burrowed into his pores.

"Thanks for the ride," she said softly. "I didn't mention that before. I should have, but I was—" She broke off, shoveled in another mouthful.

He picked up his spoon. "Tired?"

A shrug.

"Well," he said. "I guess I got my revenge by making you invite me in for dinner."

She smiled up at him. "You haven't tried it yet."

Obediently, he scooped up a bite and shoved it into his mouth. Flavors exploded on his tongue, garlic and heat and sour all mixed together with a dash of sweetness. It was delicious.

And he told her so.

Her mouth tipped up further. "And welcome to day one of the meal plan."

He froze, spoon with another bite still in his mouth.

"Yes," she teased. "I, in fact, do know what I'm doing."

Gabe extracted the utensil, set it carefully into his bowl. "Despite my actions, I never thought you didn't."

"You just thought you knew *better.*"

Since he couldn't deny that, he just nodded and went back to eating. "What's in this recipe anyway?"

She began rattling off ingredients, but it was the tofu that got him.

"Where?" He searched the bowl for the large slimy chunks.

"I used a soft tofu," she said. "As it cooks, it melts over the pilaf, making it creamy and delicious without any dairy. Plus, it adds protein."

"Well, it's probably the best thing I've ever eaten," he said, meaning it as he picked up his spoon again and did his best to get to the bottom of his bowl.

She huffed out a laugh. "You don't have to butter me up."

"Okay, so maybe it's not the *best* thing I've ever eaten," he admitted, "but it's definitely the best thing I've ever eaten with tofu in it."

"*That* I'll take."

He set down the spoon. "And also, I was a jerk about the food plan."

"We've established that already."

She wasn't going to make this easy on him. Good. "I'm hoping I can show you that I'm not normally a jerk."

"Evidence would prove otherwise," she grumbled, picking up her wineglass.

He laughed, full and deep, and when he turned to look at her, she was laughing, too, though it was softer, gentler, as though she were unused to doing it. "If I promise to not be a jerk in the future," he said, "can we be friends?"

The laughter in her expression faded. "I'm not sure that's a good idea."

He wasn't either, but there was also part of him that wouldn't let go of the idea of having some part of this woman in his life. He'd misjudged her badly, been a dick, and tried to ignore the pull he felt toward her for years now . . . and it had gotten him exactly nowhere. Now, he wanted to lean into it. And that began with proving to her he wasn't always a total asshole.

So, friends.

"Can we just try?"

She nibbled the corner of her mouth, eyes meeting his for a long moment. Then she nodded. "Okay."

Relief poured through him, and he topped off her wine before picking up both empty bowls and carrying them over to the sink. "What were you going to do before I invaded your dinner?"

Rebecca traced the top of her glass. "This. Eat. Drink some wine. Though," she said, "I *was* going to do it in my pajamas and with some bad reality television on in the background."

He turned on the water. "Go do it."

Her eyes flashed to his.

"Go, get comfortable," he said. "It's late, so I'll do the aforementioned dishes then get out of your hair."

"You don't have to—"

"I promised."

More eye contact, a longer lingering look of those gorgeous green eyes of hers.

"Go ahead," he encouraged. "Get changed. "

Eventually, she nodded and slid her chair back, bending over to light the incense on the table in an almost absent-minded moment, as though she'd done it a hundred, a thousand times before. Then she stood, shot a hesitant gaze in his direction, and crossed to a closed door, disappearing behind it.

Which was the moment he realized exactly how critical of an error he'd made.

She was taking off her clothes.

With only a flimsy wooden panel between them.

"Fuck," he muttered, washing the dishes as quickly as possible. His plan was friendship. That was the smart thing, the *only* thing, considering they worked together. But then his mind conjured up Brit and Stefan, Mandy and Blane, Kevin and the other Rebecca. They all worked together in one form or another, and their relationships were rock solid. Maybe—

Hell, who was he kidding?

Rebecca deserved better than him, better than a man who'd spent years not seeing the gem she was underneath her shyness.

Which was why he hurried to finish the dishes then made his way to the door.

Her deserving better was the *only* reason he didn't wait for her to come out, to try and catch a glimpse of her in what would no doubt be adorable—because she was in them—pajamas.

Yup. That was the sole reason he left.

And not because he was terrified that in seeing the gem underneath, he might have discovered someone he couldn't live without.

# SIX

REBECCA

She stood inside her bedroom for an obscenely long time, working up the courage to walk back out.

But she'd put on her pajamas, a baggy T-shirt and her rattiest, but also coziest sweats, and now Gabe was out there, and he'd see—

What?

At worst, a woman he couldn't stand and at best, one he'd friend-zoned.

Either way, that meant it shouldn't matter what she was wearing.

And yet, it *did* matter.

Still, Rebecca wasn't letting herself process that at the moment. In fact, she didn't really have the mental energy *to* process it, what with her trying to shore up her courage to face Gabe again.

She sucked in a breath, turned the knob, and yanked open the door to find . . .

Her apartment empty.

The first thing she noticed after realizing Gabe had gone were the two bowls resting upside down on a towel beside the sink. The next, that the Crock-Pot insert had been cleaned out as well, and was sitting next to them.

The last was . . . that she was disappointed.

She sighed, focused on the inane in order to forget all about that disappointment. There were several pictures slightly askew. She straightened them. Too much ash had accumulated in the incense tray. She'd need to remember to empty it. Gabe—

The man was thorough. That was a good thing. Of course, he'd also gone. That was less nice.

Inhaling deeply, she walked over to the couch, reaching for the blanket she always kept draped over its back, but then freezing just as her fingers grazed the organic, cruelty-free wool.

Her glass.

He'd brought it over to the coffee table for her. Further that, he had even set it on a coaster. She started to sit down, but a note tucked under the glass had her stopping.

*Don't forget to lock up.*

Rebecca's heart skipped a beat.

Tiny ways of caring.

Kryptonite. Hers.

She bit the inside of her mouth and walked to the door, throwing on the chain and engaging the dead bolt before making her way back to her blanket and her wine. But as she cued up her favorite reality show to play in the background, her mind was less on the bickering happening on screen and more focused on Gabe and his personality change.

From archnemesis—yes, the title was dramatic—to friend.

She just didn't know if it was possible. For him to be nice to her for an extended period of time, to truly mean his apology and change his behavior. For *her* to get past the walls in her mind and become friends with someone like him.

Her eyes drifted back down to the note, to the cramped hand-writing and command to be careful and lock up. She thought about the neatly stacked bowls, the clean Crock-Pot, the glass on the coaster.

Then wondered if maybe Gabe had been hiding as much of himself as she was of herself.

Those meandering musings brought her around in several circles, the fear of finding out the answer mixing with the urge to burrow in and discover the truth for certain. But in the end, she forced the thoughts from her mind and focused on the wine, on the TV, and her favorite show.

Dr. Gabe Carter was an anomaly and she had the feeling she could spend a lifetime musing about the man without discovering the truth deep inside.

All signs pointed to him being about as prepared to lay his inner works bare to observers as she was.

Which meant, of course, not at all.

It was safer that way.

———

The next morning she held a mason jar of oats in one hand and her purse in the other.

That wasn't the problem.

Nope. The *actual* issue that caused her to pause at the top of the stairs leading down to the parking lot was having forgotten she didn't have her car.

Cool.

Sighing, she tucked the jar under her arm, shoved the spoon in her pocket, and wrestled her phone out of her purse. She was opening the Lyft app when she heard the whistle.

"Yo!"

Rebecca jumped, nearly dropping everything in her hands, and whipped around to see that Gabe had parked in her spot again. He waved when her gaze made it to him.

"Need a ride?"

Her heart double-timed. Well, it was *already* double-timing from nearly being scared out of her wits, so really it quadruple-timed. "I-I—" She shook her head, animatronic bobble-head that she was, trying to find her words. But Gabe didn't press her for an answer. He waited as she sucked in a breath, shook her head again, and then eventually answered, "Sure."

That surprised her.

But then again, maybe it didn't.

Gabe was—

"Get in."

Just like last night, he didn't open the door for her, didn't help her with her bags, instead, getting in his own side and starting up the engine. Yet . . . that wasn't a bad thing. First, she could carry her own things. Second, if he'd tried to help her, she probably would have gotten all flustered and awkward and would have ended up with a jar of oats all over her favorite pair of retro jeans.

And they were awesome jeans, pale blue flowers embroidered at the seams of the pockets, so she really didn't want to have to scrub overnight oats out of them.

She opened the door, reaching in to carefully set the jar into the cup holder, then busied herself with getting her coat, purse, and backpack all stowed at her feet. But she wasn't so busy as to miss the look that Gabe gave her oats.

"Not a word," she snapped, settling herself into her seat and buckling in.

"I didn't say anything," he said, shifting the car into reverse.

"You were eyeing my oats," she said. "Don't worry, I promise not to mess up the sanctity of your car and eat within it."

He paused, checked traffic, then pulled out of the spot and onto the street. "Contrary to some people, I don't consider my car my personal sanctuary. I have even been known—gasp—to eat the occasional fast food meal within it."

"So, unlike Cooper."

She watched the corner of his mouth twitch. "Yes, unlike Cooper."

Their newest player was known for his obsession with keeping his cars pristine, and the rules about riding in them were apparently endless. *Or* they might be relatively minimal—no eating or drinking—to nonexistent—an offhand comment mentioned once. Regardless, it was the thing the rest of the team had decided to tease him about and so it had taken on a whole life of its own.

They hit the on-ramp for the freeway and then made their way through the typical morning stop and go. Traffic in the Bay Area was some of the worst in the nation, and lucky her, she got to experience it most mornings.

But she couldn't complain too much. She lived in California. The weather was amazing, the food options, especially for a vegan, varied and delicious, and she had easy access to beaches and mountains.

When she worked up the courage to vary her routine and go see them that was.

And she did.

Work up the courage *and* went to visit them.

Just not when it was snowing.

Driving through the white fluffy stuff, she had not yet conquered.

Or rain. Or not being a nervous wreck when she was in a car with—

"Did you enjoy your pajamas last night?"

She blinked, realized she'd been daydreaming about snow and rain and beaches and mountains for several minutes. Biting her lip, she risked a look at Gabe. His eyes flicked to hers then back to the road. He didn't seem upset that she'd drifted off to her own mental world.

"Yes," she murmured. "What'd you do after you left last night?"

"Went home," he said and shrugged. "Had a beer. Crashed."

"Where's home?"

"Not far from you, actually," he said and told her an address that was on the waterfront just a few minutes away from hers.

"So, what do you think the chances are of the guys adhering to your plan?"

Rebecca glanced at him, wondering if he was going to start in on her about the diet. Instead, he kept talking.

"Because if there is any doubt, I'd think all you had to do was feed them what you fed me last night."

Oh.

*Oh.*

"You really liked it?"

"My practically licking the bowl didn't give that away?"

She smiled.

"I think it's wise you plan on meeting with all of the players to personalize it. Means they're more likely to be on board."

She nodded. "Yes. I'm sure there will be some who won't, but I can't tie them down and force them to only eat what I want them to."

"As much as you'd prefer to do that," he said with a laugh.

Since she couldn't exactly deny that, Rebecca didn't bother. Instead, she changed the subject. "How did you end up with the Gold?"

He maneuvered over a lane. "That's a boring story," he said, voice completely devoid of emotion.

That answer was enough for her to know the story was far from boring.

"I thought we were going to try and be friends."

Gabe took the exit that led to the rink. "We *are* friends."

"Well," she said. "Friends don't let friends get away with vague answers. Especially vague answers that are deliberately vague about important things."

"I thought you were supposed to be shy."

At one time, or with another person that might have made her shut down, to get quiet and nervous, but she wasn't like that with Gabe. With him, all the extra noise in her brain, the insecurities and the what ifs and fears, were gone.

It was just her and him.

So, she was able to recognize he was teasing her. And miraculously, she was able to joke back.

"I thought all you doctors were supposed to love expounding on yourselves and your great accomplishments."

He laughed. "I knew she was there."

Rebecca frowned. "Knew *who* was there?"

"You. This." He pulled into the parking lot of the rink. "I knew you'd be feisty underneath."

Feisty.

Now she could honestly say that was a word no one had ever used to describe her.

"Don't get quiet on me now," he murmured, pulling into a spot. "I like feisty Rebecca."

She picked up the jar of oats she'd been too busy talking to eat. "I have anxiety," she said, playing with the top, running her finger over the bumps on the shiny metal lid. "I've had it my whole life."

Silence.

Then, "I know, sweetheart."

Her breath caught.

"I should have known sooner, should have realized that was why you acted the way you did sometimes."

"I can be a pain in the ass," she agreed with a shrug. Or at least, that's what her sister always said.

"And that's different from anyone else how?" He rotated to face her. "Because as far as I can tell, you've witnessed *my* pain in the ass multiple times."

"I—" Her mouth opened and closed. "Well, yes."

A laugh. "And here's the thing. I'm a doctor. I should have realized you were struggling. I should have helped rather than—"

That pissed her off. "I don't *need* help," she snapped. "I'm fine. I've been in therapy for a decade. I have ways to cope, ways to push through. I've gotten this far without—"

He rested his hand lightly on hers. "I didn't mean it like that."

He sighed. "I created a work environment that made it harder for you when I should have—"

"I don't need people going around and making my life easier. I'm not weak."

His fingers squeezed. "I know that."

"I'm good at my job. I don't want someone to make allowances for me."

"I know that, too," he said gently. "However, we're supposed to be a team, one that I'm in charge of. And the sign of any good leader is being able to pull out the best in their teammates. I didn't do that."

"You didn't *have*—"

Another squeeze. "Do you think we can agree to disagree on this?"

Rebecca paused. Sighed. Then, "Fine."

"Good, because despite the fight I put up during the process, I like your plan and I like you."

"I-I—" What the hell could she say to that? He'd said it once before, but she'd assumed it was anger talking and had put it out of her mind. He couldn't like her. Not when she was who she was and he was . . . Gabe.

But this?

This was offered up casually, as though it weren't a big deal to declare such a thing.

"You can't be surprised," he murmured. "I did tell you that at Kevin and Bex's party."

"You growled it at me," she said.

He considered that. "Yes, that's true. And because of that, you thought I was lying?"

"Not lying, exactly . . ." Okay, so *yes,* lying. Or maybe purposefully choosing the wrong words because he was annoyed.

"Not lying," he said. "Exactly, or otherwise. I'm a good guy. You're a cool chick. I just know it's going to take time for you to accept both of those facts as truth."

Thankfully, Gabe didn't seem to expect a response. He

popped open his car door, got out, and this time rounded the hood to pull hers wide. Her backpack went over his shoulder as she was scooping up her purse and climbing out.

"I can—"

"You should probably call Triple A to look at your car. They might take a while to come out."

"You're right—"

"I also found a few other research papers I think you might find helpful for the meal plan stuff. You probably have already read them, but a colleague sent them over, and I thought you might enjoy—"

"Gabe. Blinders."

He blinked.

"Conversational this time."

His mouth twitched. "Sorry."

She closed the door, snagged her backpack. "Don't apologize."

"Okay."

"I'd like those papers."

"Okay."

"And to keep being friends."

He bumped her shoulder with his, and she tried to ignore the zing the contact sent down her spine. "Okay."

"But only if you stop saying okay."

A shrug. "Okay."

She smacked him. He laughed. They walked into the rink together, talking about the plan for the team and upcoming events with the staff. It wasn't entirely free of awkward, she still occasionally got quiet and shy, but when she looked back, that conversation marked the beginning of her friendship with Gabe.

It also marked the end of her life as she knew it.

# SEVEN

## GABE

He knocked on Rebecca's office door.

It was partially closed and the panel glided inward at the contact.

Which meant he caught her red-handed. Or maybe red-wrappered? Since she was shoving a large piece of chocolate into her mouth.

He grinned and walked in, plunking himself into the chair in front of her desk and loving the flush of pink on her cheeks. "I thought you didn't eat sugar?"

She chewed and swallowed. "I—uh—" That jerky shake of her head.

"I'm teasing. Pomegranate with honey. From Molly's," Gabe said and set the to-go cup of tea he'd picked up for her on the desk, having bummed the name of her favorite place and drink from Mandy. She'd given him a knowing look, and he knew asking would no doubt garner him no end of shit from the guys. Worth it, though, to see Rebecca's smile.

"I don't eat *refined* sugar," she said, holding up the wrapper. "And this is actually sweetened with honey. See?"

He took the foiled paper, giving it a cursory look before sticking it in his pocket.

For later consideration.

She picked up the cup, smiled shyly at him. "Thanks."

God, she was pretty and warm. How had he missed the warm before? Oh yeah, because he'd taken one look at her, panicked and then amplified every negative he could find about her.

Which was basically nothing.

So yeah, lots of ass-hattery to make up for.

She started telling him how Mandy had recommended the brand, saying that no woman should have to do without choco-late—which was totally something Mandy would say—when her cell buzzed.

He started to stand, but she just glanced at the screen and silenced it.

"No, it's okay," she said. "It's my sister, and those calls are never short. I'll catch her later."

He nodded, sat, and silence descended.

Teeth nibbling on the corner of her mouth, she murmured, "Thanks again for the tea."

"No problem."

"D-do you have any family?" The question was abrupt and blurted out.

He sucked in a breath.

Rebecca flushed. "You don't have to answer that," she said quickly. "My parents are both alive but divorced. It's just that my sister is much older than me and sometimes it seems like I have three parents because of it."

"A lot of pressure."

"Definitely a lot of *opinions*." Her lips quirked. "Mom moved to a small town, knows everyone there, and the pace of life is slow and easy. It's perfect for her. My dad and sister live in L.A. now. Fast living, lots of business opportunities, and judgment aplenty. Perfect for them."

He nodded then shared, "My parents are gone. Lost dad

about five years ago. Mom, while I was in college. No siblings, but I had a group of close friends growing up."

Until they'd lost Maggie.

Then they'd drifted apart.

"Mandy and the team are the closest thing I have to a family now."

She touched his hand. "I'm sorry."

"I'm not," he said. "This isn't the worst place to have a family."

She smiled. "No, I'm starting to see that it's not."

---

He glanced up at the knock on *his* office door.

Rebecca was standing there with pink cheeks and uncertain eyes. It had been a week since they formed their tentative friendship, and he'd been dropping off daily doses of chocolate and pomegranate tea.

But this was the first time she'd come to him.

"Hey," she said. "I was just going to grab a salad at Molly's. Do you want me to get you something?"

He set down the file and stood. "I'll come with you."

"Oh no, you don't have to."

Gabe snagged his jacket and wallet. "I've been sitting at my desk all morning so could use a chance to stretch my legs. Unless you don't want company?"

She hesitated then, "No. Company would be welcome."

"Okay." He gestured for her to precede him, and they walked down the hall in not quite comfortable silence. But it wasn't *un*comfortable, so he thought that was a marked improvement.

Mandy poked her head out as they walked by, mouth opening then closing before she lifted a brow.

He narrowed his eyes at her, but she just smiled innocently, giving him a finger wave.

More gossip for the mill.

Rebecca smiled up at him. "I'm buying you lunch, just so you know."

"I *don't* know that."

A roll of her eyes. "You've bought me tea every day this week, not to mention the chocolate you snuck into my desk drawer. The least I can do is get you a sandwich or something."

"I can buy my own lunch."

She plunked her hands on her hips. "And I can buy my own tea. I'm trying to be nice here."

Spice.

Yup. He liked it a lot.

Rebecca huffed, and he couldn't help it. He smiled.

Which she caught, of course. "Oh, lord. You're teasing me, aren't you?"

"Busted." Another grin. "But I will allow you to buy me lunch."

"Too late. Offer's off the table," she grumbled.

He caught the end of her red ponytail and tugged lightly. "It's fun teasing you, especially when you give it back."

She rolled her eyes, but her lips were twitching. "Fine. I'll buy you a sandwich, but you have a ten-dollar limit."

He laughed, and together they walked to Molly's.

———

It was Friday night and he'd convinced Rebecca to come out with him after they'd both been caught up at work late.

He'd been walking her to her car when her stomach had rumbled, so had bribed her with chocolate and a vegan restaurant he'd looked up online. But she'd surprised him by suggesting they go see the latest Marvel movie instead.

Apparently, she hadn't gotten around to seeing this one yet.

He never would have picked her for an action movie fan, but then again, she seemed to be a professional at surprising him.

They sat side by side in the reclining seats and he couldn't remember the last time he'd been to the movies with a woman and it hadn't been a date. Maybe with Mandy when they'd first moved here? But definitely not since then. Usually, he took dates to fancy restaurants, not kid-filled movie theaters.

Still, it wasn't all bad. He was, after all, sitting next to Rebecca, her cinnamon and floral scent drifting across the air to his nose. That smell was quickly becoming a comfort.

Or maybe addicting.

Both.

Yeah, it was both.

There wasn't any butter on his popcorn—because Rebecca was a vegan—which normally he'd call a crime against humanity, but because she was there with him, it was totally fine. She was eating a salad they'd picked up from Molly's on the way in. He'd stuck with a hot dog and other traditional movie snacks, to which she'd shook her head, but hadn't said a word.

"Mom!" came a young voice from the row behind them, trailing the sound of crinkling and food hitting the ground.

"Shh," he guessed the mom in question said.

"But Bethany spilled the popcorn!"

"Luckily, we had enough."

"But I'm still hungry."

"Hush," she whispered. "The movie's on."

"But—"

"Luke," she said, still whispering. "I just spent a hundred dollars on tickets for us all and food for you both. I don't have any more mon—"

The preview on the screen debuted with a loud bang.

Rebecca slid from her seat. "Be right back."

He nodded, debating whether he should offer to buy the family behind him a fresh bag of popcorn. San Francisco, in general, was expensive and having kids in the city even more so.

But would that make him an eavesdropping asshole?

Maybe he should offer them some of their bag.

Yeah, that wasn't creepy at all. Thirty-something white dude offers treats to children in the dark. Couldn't go wrong.

Another preview came on, and he decided that he'd go buy them a fresh bag when Rebecca came back. But then another one started and there was still no sign of her. Finally, when he was just starting to worry, she came walking up the aisle.

But she didn't come to their row.

Instead, she passed by then slid between the chairs behind him until she reached the mom and kids and whispered, "This is for you guys."

"Oh no, I couldn't possibly," the mom said softly, and they spent half a minute arguing over the fresh bag of popcorn. Eventually, however, the mom relented with a teary sounding, "Thank you," and Rebecca came back to find her seat.

He squeezed her hand as the movie began.

She squeezed back.

Then didn't let go.

# Eight

REBECCA

The phone rang as she was neck-deep in Yelp reviews for the restaurant Gabe had suggested.

She glanced at the screen, saw it was her sister Sandra, and sighed.

She'd been avoiding this call for the last week, which was the upper limit on what her sister would allow before she flew up to the city and cornered Rebecca at work.

She knew this from experience.

So. Much. Fun.

Her cell rang again, and she answered the call. "Hey, sis."

"What's wrong?" Sandra snapped in a tone that made her jump.

"What do you mean?"

"You're avoiding my calls. That means something is wrong."

Rebecca rolled her eyes. "I'm not avoiding your calls"—lie—"I'm just busy with work"—truth—"I'm rolling out a new diet plan and—"

"The team bought into your woo-woo food ideas, huh?"

That stung, but she kept her tone even. "That's what they hired me for."

"People do crazy things all the time," Sandra quipped then laughed, like Rebecca was laughing alongside her. But she didn't laugh with her sister. Instead, she felt numb to the comments. After a lifetime of them from her dad and Sandra, it was hard to work up any sort of useful outrage.

Especially when Sandra always managed to be outraged enough for the both of them.

"Yup," she said instead. "They sure do."

"What's your therapist say about the job?"

"That she's happy I found something I enjoy and am good at."

Sandra snorted. "Happy. That's an interesting way to put it. She help you work up the courage to move down to L.A. yet?"

God no.

That wasn't happening. Ever.

Four hundred and fifty miles between her sister, her dad, and herself was just about perfect.

"I—"

A knock interrupted her.

"Of course not," Sandra said, taking the pause as Rebecca struggling with words. And maybe sometimes it was. Just not this time. But she launched into a story of an intern getting decaf coffee instead of regular coffee as Rebecca walked to the door to answer it.

How terrible.

She rolled her eyes and glanced through the peephole, unlocking the dead bolt and letting Gabe in.

"There's someone at my door. I've got to go."

"You have a date?"

It was Friday night, so not an unreasonable assumption, unless of course, someone considered the complete shock in her sister's tone.

"No," Rebecca said, kind of wishing she could answer the

opposite. Not that it would ever happen. Not between her and Gabe. "I'm going out to dinner with a friend. I'll talk to you soon, okay, Sandra?"

"Don't avoid my calls."

She purposefully didn't agree to that. "Bye."

Gabe studied her face carefully. "Sister?"

"Yeah."

"In parent mode again?"

Her heart pulsed, knowing he'd sized up her mood just that quickly. "Yeah."

He bumped her shoulder with his. "Know what the cure for that is?"

"What?"

"Cashew cheese."

She laughed. "My favorite."

Gabe helped her into her jacket and then they drove down to the restaurant. He had her in stitches gossiping about Mandy and Blane being caught making out in a supply closet of all places, then had her searching her old anatomy and physiology knowledge as they discussed several of his ideas for treatment plans for a few of the guys. By the time they'd arrived at the restaurant, she'd relaxed enough to not panic being at a new place, not knowing where the bathrooms were or what she was going to order.

They made it to a booth without issue and she stayed relaxed.

It was easy with Gabe.

He stripped away all the parts that made her falter and just let it be the two of them. It was lovely and peaceful and . . . perfect.

So much so that she even ordered something that hadn't been described in the Yelp reviews.

———

"I don't know how I let you talk me into these things," she declared, doing her best impression of a baby deer on ice skates.

Well, she *was* on skates.

She just had two legs instead of four.

But she still didn't think that four legs would have helped.

Gabe laughed and glided past her, executing a spin that was way too graceful for her liking.

Especially since she was clinging to the boards.

He came back and slid an arm around her waist, tugging her from the safety of the plastic barrier.

"Gabe! No!"

"I've got you," he said, leading her over to where Mandy and Blane were holding hands at center ice.

"I'm going to murder you with tofu."

He laughed loudly, drawing the attention of most everyone on the ice. Which was pretty much the entire team, since they were at a Gold family event that included ice skating and Sutter, the Miner—the team's semi-cute, semi-maniacal-looking mascot, along with hot chocolate and cookies. She didn't miss the raised brows from the guys and their spouses, nor did she miss the fact that there had been absolutely no talk about her and Gabe maybe being a couple.

Probably because it was obvious he wasn't interested in her that way.

Internally, she wrinkled her nose, not sure she liked how that notion made her feel, but also knowing there was no helping it.

Friends.

That was what he wanted.

Even if they seemed to be spending most of their free evenings together.

He took them around in several slow circles, navigating around the kiddos and especially wide of Brayden, Max's rambunctious son, who was hell on two blades, before she cried off. Her ankles were killing her.

Gabe led her to the open Zamboni doors and back down the hall to the pair of chairs where they'd left their shoes.

Her hands felt frozen, along with her nose.

This is what growing up in California did to a person.

She fumbled with numb fingers, trying to undo the laces before Gabe saved her again, kneeling down in front of her and helping her take them off.

"Thanks," she murmured, curling and uncurling her toes.

"So, not going to take up hockey?" he asked, setting the skates to the side and climbing into the chair next to her so he could remove his own.

"That's a no," she said. "But thanks for helping me. I won't say that was fun exactly, though I did enjoy seeing everyone out there."

And him.

She'd enjoyed spending the evening with him.

But she didn't say that because . . . friends.

Sighing, she slipped her feet into her shoes and began doing up the laces. When she straightened, he was studying her closely. "You okay?"

"Great," she mumbled.

His finger brushed down her cheek and she shivered.

"You're cold," he said, standing and bustling around for a few seconds to return the skates then came back and snagged her hand. He had her down the hall and into his office in less than a minute, tossing the coat he kept there over her shoulders.

The garment might have warmed her skin, but the gesture had already warmed her from the inside out.

Thus was the appeal of Dr. Gabe Carter.

Sigh.

Friends. They were *just* friends.

———

Reality TV and wine.

And Gabe.

He grinned over at her when she gasped, unable to believe what had just happened on screen.

She whipped to face him. "Seriously?"

"Apparently so." His shoulders lifted and fell. "I can't believe those girls laughed at his jokes. They were lame."

"Takes one to know one?" she teased, picking up her wine glass and lifting it to her lips.

He tipped the bottom up lightly, so she had to gulp in a sip.

Swallowing quickly, she glared.

He laughed.

She laughed.

They both settled back and kept watching. At least until there was a knock on the door. Frowning, she started to rise to see who was there. He stopped her with a hand on her thigh—and cue butterflies she definitely shouldn't be feeling.

"It's just dinner," he said. "I DoorDashed in from Molly's."

"Gabe!"

He shrugged and stood, moving to answer the knock. Thirty seconds later, he was back with a bag.

"You promised *I'd* get the next one."

"Meh," he said. "I was hungry, and you were on the phone. Just get me next time."

Sandra's fault because . . . more nagging about going to L.A.

Gabe opened the lid and handed over her favorite salad—mixed greens with a raspberry vinaigrette and candied walnuts—then picked up his own.

"You said that last time, too," she reminded him.

He picked up the remote. "It doesn't matter—"

"It matters to me! I don't want to mooch—"

"Not mooching. I like taking care of you." Her breath caught at the flash of heat in his eyes, but before she could convince herself it was there, he turned back to the TV and pressed play to start the show.

Still, the words alone had her heart pounding.

She liked it when he took care of her, too, liked taking care of him back.

The on-screen argument heated up, various parties yelling at each other over odd metal wine glasses.

Salad. Gabe. TV.

Yeah, this was the life.

But she couldn't deny the blip of disappointment she felt when Gabe said into a lull in the argument. "Friends take care of each other, right?"

She sighed and speared a walnut.

Friends.

Right.

# NINE

## GABE

"I-I'm sorry," she said. "I don't think it's a good idea if we go on a date."

"It doesn't have to be a date," a male voice he recognized as Cooper's said. "We can just go out for drinks. Take a little time to get to know—"

Gabe froze three steps from the open door to Rebecca's office, gut churning, heart pounding.

He'd friend-zoned himself.

He'd spent the last four months getting to know Rebecca, understanding all the things that made her tick, proving to her—and himself—that he wasn't an asshole.

Which were good things, *great* things, but also . . . blue balls.

As in, he'd given himself perpetual ones.

But now, he'd waited too long to take what was his.

"If those drinks involve other people, then . . . maybe," Rebecca murmured. "But o-otherwise I-I—"

Gabe's heart skipped a beat, and he realized he hadn't heard her stammer around him for months. And he didn't like the uncertainty in her tone, the way it seemed devoid of spice and fire.

Luckily, Coop was a good guy. He'd realized she wasn't having it, and said, "No worries. Maybe we can grab something with Mandy and Blane and Kevin and Bex sometime."

Rebecca's sigh of relief was audible even in the hall. "Thanks for understanding," she replied. "I'd like that."

"Thank you for creating such a good diet plan that I feel about ten years younger." A beat. "Minus those gray hairs Max is giving me by discussing the copious amount of gloriousness that is *The Witcher*."

She giggled. "Thanks for offering to be my phase two guinea pig."

"With the food you've cooked, I can honestly say it hasn't been a trial."

"O-oh, it's not a big deal. I—"

"Maybe not, but I appreciate it anyway," Coop said before calling out a goodbye and coming out into the hall. The brief hard look Gabe gave him and the short, terse nod Coop gave in return told Gabe everything he needed to know. Coop had gotten the message and wouldn't continue pursuing her.

Good.

Rebecca was his.

If only he could figure out a way for her to realize that without her panicking on him and retreating. That was why he'd endured four months of friend-zoning and blue balls. Because she deserved patience and care . . . but also because he was terrified that if he pushed, all the progress they'd made together would be gone like so much smoke.

Maybe cowardly, but at least being friends meant he had her in his life.

She smiled up at him as he knocked on her doorframe, cheeks still pink from Coop's visit, but her eyes filled with relief. It was the end of the workday, the first time she'd been back in the office after attending a conference in San Diego, and yet it was as pristine as always. Her desktop was clear, the baskets on it perfectly straight and filled with color-coordinated files. Still as organized as ever. The difference now was that he understood what it meant, how the stringent system meant that she could do her job without getting bogged down with anxiety.

"Hi," she murmured, plunking her highlighter back into the cup that sat next to her keypad. "I didn't think I'd see you until tomorrow."

He shrugged. "The team's plane got in early, so I came in to catch up on some work."

Lie. He'd come in to see her.

Because he'd spent the last four months falling in love with her.

And she had absolutely no clue.

Pathetic.

"Do you want to grab a bite to eat?" she asked, not mentioning Cooper, for which he was grateful. "I was just finishing up for the day, and I am starving."

Also reason one thousand and one for why he wasn't pushing: he got invites like this while men like Coop didn't. He got to sit across from her in a restaurant studying her, hearing her soft laughter at his jokes, sharing some of his own when she gave it back, witnessing her bloom with joy over wine and food. For a woman with a fairly restrictive diet—no sugar, no caffeine, no meat or dairy—she sure loved food.

And he fucking loved watching her enjoy it.

Those little moans she'd made while chowing down on cauliflower and cashew mac n cheese and gluten-free, vegan, cardamom-rose cake at the small restaurant off Market they'd eaten at the previous week were imprinted onto his brain.

No clue. Rebecca had absolutely no clue how beautiful she was.

Or sexy.

"You sure you want to tolerate my presence?" he teased, when she glanced up at him with concern in her eyes.

Her head tilted to the side and his breath caught when he got a lot of those pretty green eyes. That had been happening more and more, but it never failed to make his lungs seize, the rare gift of her looking closely at him.

Because he knew how tough it was for her.

And he knew how few people she felt comfortable doing it with.

"Are you okay?"

"I'm great," he said, jaw clenching in an effort to stifle the need to go to her, to take her in his arms, and—

"Gabe."

"I'm fine," he said and admitted the truth—or *well*, something in the realm of truth. "I'm just tired."

Tired of having part of Rebecca when he wanted more. Tired of men like Coop thinking she was available when he wanted to brand his name across her forehead. Tired of treading carefully but knowing he must.

"Yeah." A beat of silence. "But let it be known, you're my friend," she eventually said. "Which means I always want to spend time with you."

Friend. *Fuck.*

He spun around, facing the hall and trying to get himself under control. He only had himself to blame for this predicament. He'd been the one to declare them friends, had shoved his whole  alpha-I-like-you-too-much-and-now-I'm-going-to-claim-you urges under the rug, and focused on keeping everything light and breezy.

Because she'd needed that.

Not him pushing his way into her life, like some sort of possessive twat-waffle. She'd needed consideration, kindness, someone to rely on, rather than a man who wanted to own every part of her.

Let it be known to the universe at large that he *was* possessive. He *did* want to own every part.

Rebecca grabbed her purse. He knew she did because he'd spent the last months learning everything about her. So, he knew the exact sound of her desk drawer sliding open, the squeak of her chair pushing back so she could reach down and grab her bag. The next thing she'd do was slip her shoes on and then stretch her neck out, right to left, right to left.

Then she'd pick up her backpack and move past him into the hall, the scent of cinnamon trailing her as she walked.

*Patience. This is a long game.* He stifled a sigh, wondering how much longer this long game would be, and focused on the present. "Want to try that place on—" Her shoulder brushed his as she shifted in front of him instead of going into the hall.

"Gabe." She cupped his cheek. "What's wrong?"

They'd touched before. Over their four months of friendship, it would have been unbelievable for it to be otherwise. But those accidental brushes, the pats of the hand and shoulder weren't *this*.

And *she'd* never touched him first.

Never.

Now the soft skin of her palm brushing along his jaw was the most intense sensation he'd ever experienced. His nerves went from quiescent to on fire in the span of a heartbeat as heat flared down his spine.

"I'm fine," he rasped. "Just tired."

She stepped closer, her breasts brushing his chest.

He sucked in a breath.

Rebecca rose on tiptoe and her mouth. Was. Right. There. "Gabe?"

He lost it, lost any semblance of his remaining control. His hands came up to grip her upper arms, some part of his mind intending to push her away, while the remainder knew he could never manage to distance this woman in any way.

Not now. Not after all this time.

Her lips parted, asking again, "G-Gabe?"

That stutter did him in. His head dropped, and he pressed his mouth to hers.

# TEN

REBECCA

He was kissing her.

Gabe was kissing her.

*Oh fucking hell, he was kissing her!*

She froze, her mind full of swirling thoughts. Had he made a mistake? Maybe his mouth had accidentally fallen onto hers? Should she back away? No. She shouldn't be ridiculous. *Of course,* his mouth hadn't fallen on hers. He was kissing her. But did that mean she should kiss him back? What if he didn't like the way she did it?

All of that was whipping through her mind and so it took her a moment to realize that Gabe was pulling back.

*God, no.*

She didn't want him to stop.

The thoughts quieted, her purse dropped to the floor with a thump, and her hands came up, fingers weaving into the hair on his nape as she brought her mouth back to his.

They'd spent four months together, and most of that time she'd been fantasizing about this moment, when she finally got up the courage to do what was happening, to act on her feelings, feelings that had been building from the moment he apologized for being a jerk then had insinuated himself into her life.

They ate more meals together than apart. They went to movies together. Had gone wine tasting and to the ocean. She'd even turned him on to one of her favorite reality shows.

They were friends.

But nothing more.

And she'd thought that was what he wanted, so she hadn't dared to wish for more.

Didn't dare to hope she could find a way to offer him more.

Not when her anxiety sometimes made day-to-day stuff impossible.

It had taken three cancelations and date changes before they'd finally made it to the beach, a long research process of the winery and how the tours operated before she'd agreed to go, and multiple instances of Yelp review trolling before she was willing to try a new restaurant.

But she'd gone.

She'd gone and she'd had fun and it hadn't gotten easier so much as the world she'd gotten comfortable experiencing had expanded.

Because of Gabe.

Who was never impatient but always encouraging.

Who made her wish that the lonely future she'd always imagined might include a friend like Gabe.

But she'd never imagined it could include him like *this*.

With his lips against hers, his chest pressed to her breasts, the warmth of his body seeping into hers.

She'd been kissed before, and it had *never* been like this.

Her body was on fire, but her mind was finally calm, just soaking in the sensations rather than trying to analyze everything. *Feel not think.* Her therapist had mentioned to her more than once, one of the many techniques to keep in her back pocket to help her live her life. But she'd never understood it, not until that moment. Because her feelings *were* what was terrifying, what stopped her from living her life, prevented her from doing things she wanted to or had to or *needed* to do.

She'd needed to feel less, not more.

Except . . . now she understood.

It wasn't so much emotions her therapist had wanted her to focus on, rather, she should immerse herself in how her body felt —heart pounding, head spinning, desire spiraling. She should allow her fingers to revel in the soft silk of his hair against her skin, the spicy scent soaking into her nostrils.

*That* was feeling.

And it was incredible.

But it was also fleeting because Gabe eventually pulled back, his hands drifting gently down the outsides of her arms and making her shiver. "Are you okay?" he asked, voice husky and eyes hot.

She nodded, her own words stoppered up in the back of her throat. What had happened was a lot, bordering on almost too much. And it was also exceptional. Perfect. The best kiss of her life.

"Kind of need to hear you say the words, sweetheart."

"What words?" she asked. "I-I don't know what to say other than that it was incredible, Gabe. I—" She stumbled to a stop, not understanding what he wanted. It was perfect, hot as hell, but—

"You're not overwhelmed?"

She snorted. Of course, she was overwhelmed. That kiss had been everything. "Are *you?*"

"Yes." He smiled. "And that'll do, honey," he murmured, cupping her cheek lightly before bending to pick up her purse and handing it to her. Then he reached for her backpack, sliding it off her shoulder and onto his own.

For the first time ever, she let him carry that burden without protest.

Perhaps because instinctively she understood that this was a man who could help her shoulder her burdens.

Or more likely, because his kiss had addled her.

Regardless, when he took her hand and suggested they eat at a new restaurant without her using her ninja sleuth skills to Yelp the hell out of it, she agreed without protest. With Gabe by her side, it was easier to step outside of her carefully laid boundaries.

Especially if he kept smiling down at her like he'd done when she said yes.

Yup. Definitely addled.

That was for damn sure.

———

"Gabe?" she asked as he drove them out of the parking lot.

"Yeah?"

She nibbled at the corner of her mouth then figured, in for a penny, in for a pound. "What does it mean?"

Silence then, "What does *what* mean?"

"*Gabe,*" she warned

He pulled to the side of the road and turned to face her. "It means what you want it to be, Rebecca."

It wasn't a rejection, but those words were still a gut punch.

And . . . it was putting the pressure on her to identify what was happening between them.

"That's not fair."

"I don't want to force you to—"

"What? Kiss you?" she asked, turning in her seat as well, wanting to see his face, his eyes. And if that right there didn't tell her how far she'd come, then she didn't know what could. "I liked it," she said. "I liked kissing you. What I *don't* like is not understanding where this came from. For four months—"

"I've been pretending I didn't want you."

Her lungs froze. "You were *pretending*?" Sick. She was going to be sick.

"No, sweetheart," Gabe said, snagging her wrists when she would have leaned back in her seat. "No, not like that. But I *was* pretending that I didn't want you. I didn't want to pressure you to—"

She shrieked.

It was a legit shriek and also a sound she hadn't made in approximately twenty years. Not since she was a hormonal teenager who'd been prone to shrieking in frustration.

But, dammit, it *wasn't* fair.

"No, Gabe," she said. "You don't get to do that. You don't get to tell me you want friendship and then pull the rug out from underneath me. You don't get to pretend to want me only as a buddy one moment and then kiss the daylights out of me the next."

"I wanted to give you time," he said.

She sucked in a breath, held it for a moment, then released it. "I understand that. I appreciate it. But I'm not broken."

Funny how until she'd said the words aloud, she'd never believed them.

She wasn't broken.

She was imperfect, yes.

But so was everyone.

She *wasn't* broken.

"I've wanted you from the moment I pulled my head out of my ass four months ago," Gabe said. "But I didn't think it was fair for me to be a dick one minute then try to get in your pants the next. You deserved someone taking the time to get to know you, to see the wonderful person you are when you forget to be shy."

"I needed four *months* of that?"

He grinned. "So, maybe four months was overkill?"

She snorted. "Yeah, about three months too many."

"It *was* a long time," he said and tugged on a strand of her hair. "But honestly . . ."

"What?" she pressed when he hesitated.

"*Honestly*, if I'd approached you four—or three—months ago, would you have been open to dating me?"

Her lips parted, an agreement on the tip of her tongue, but

the words wouldn't come. Because he was right. It had taken her four months to learn him as a friend, to understand how wonderful he was, to feel comfortable enough to not freak out because he'd kissed her.

"Are you even open to dating me *now?*"

She froze, bit her lip. Was she? Could she really be like she was and have a relationship with someone? Especially when that someone was as important to her as Gabe had become?

He chucked her under the chin. "Is this where I get to say I'm right?"

She lightly smacked his hand away. "It's where you get to drive, and I get to think."

"I can do that."

Rebecca knew he could.

She knew he could do a lot of things, including peeling back the layers of her shyness and fear and anxiety, and coaxing her forward into finally living a full life.

Thus was the power of Dr. Gabe Carter.

The only question was . . . could *she* follow through?

# ELEVEN

## GABE

It was over cashew cheese—and Gabe was man enough to admit that he'd developed a liking for the vegan delicacy—that Rebecca finally met his eyes.

She hadn't been avoiding them, per se, so much as being so into whatever thoughts were going through her head that her gaze hadn't much drifted up past her menu or plate or hands. When he'd ordered for her, she'd given him a brief smile, though those eyes were still distant, and the same went for when their server had brought their food and drinks.

Aware of the outside world and yet not really.

But he didn't mind the quiet. He'd come to appreciate the fact that Rebecca didn't need to fill the silence with conversation.

"Gabe," she murmured, then immediately bit her lip, worry creeping into the edges of her expression.

"I know four months was a long time." He reached across the table to take her hands in his. "We've spent a lot of time getting to know each other," he murmured. "We were both careful, and that was a good thing."

Head tilting to the side, she asked, "Careful how?"

"Careful to keep things light between us. To get to know each other slowly and easily without bringing up a lot of the stuff that" —a squeeze—"would have complicated the process." She frowned and so he hurried on. "I've spent more time with you than most women in my life, and yet I don't know much about your upbringing or family. I know your preferred type of tea, the brand of chocolate you indulge in. I know that you dislike orange juice with pulp even though it's better for you, and I know your favorite pair of jeans is embroidered with tiny blue flowers." His heart was pounding, but he kept talking. "I know so much about you, and yet I don't know the why."

She turned her hands over in his, lacing their fingers together. That worry no longer just on the edges of her face. "It's all been superficial."

Gabe winced. "No. I didn't mean—"

A shake of her head. "Sorry, poor word choice. I understand it's important you know the small things, and I agree that I know the same about you. I guess . . . I mean, we both shared the stuff we were willing, but a lot of our walls are still there."

"Yes." He couldn't argue with that.

She sighed. "I don't know if I can do this, Gabe."

His heart sank and he started to lean back, fingers separating.

"No," she said, tilting forward, keeping their hands together. "I don't mean it like that. You're wonderful. I just—" Her gaze dropped to the table. "I never thought I would be able to be in a relationship."

"What? How?" He released one hand, cupped her cheek. "You're beautiful and smart and—"

"Have crippling anxiety," she murmured. "Don't forget *that* fact. I should think it's one you're well-familiar with by now."

"I—"

"Therapy helped. I've gotten a lot better," she said. "The life I'm living right now is bigger than I could have ever imagined, and part of that is because *you* expanded it. My job, my friends, you. I . . . didn't think I'd ever have that."

"But—"

"I don't think I've ever met a man who I've wanted to spend so much time with," she murmured. "I can *talk* to you." She laughed. "*Me.* The person who sometimes struggles to get out a sentence if it doesn't revolve around plant proteins and cashew cheese. I can just sit down at a restaurant I've never been to and talk and eat and enjoy it."

"That's a good thing, sweetheart. I'm glad I can do that with you."

Rebecca's head jerked. "But don't you see? It's *because* of you. Because we've taken this time and slowly gotten to know each other that I *can* do it. If you hadn't—" Another jerk. "I-I would still—"

"That's what people do," he said. "They take their time to learn one another."

"And it takes four months?" she asked.

"Four months isn't that long a time."

She rolled her eyes. "It is if you spend part of almost every day together."

"Okay, I'll give you that," he said. "But it's not just you or your anxiety that's made us move slowly. I haven't exactly been open to something deeper myself."

"And I don't know why." She pulled away, covering her forehead with her hands. "If you were pretending for so long to not want something when you really do want it, then how do I know you're not pretending to want me now when really you want something, *someone* whole and undamaged and easy?" She blew out a breath. "I didn't know that you wanted more, Gabe. I had absolutely no clue, and that it's been happening for four months . . .?"

His stomach was in knots. He understood where she was coming from and yet had no clue how to move past it.

"It just doesn't make any sense, Gabe."

He knew it didn't, knew it was confusing and a little scary —because he was feeling those things, too. He was quiet for a long moment then said the only thing he could, "Do you trust me?"

Her hands dropped to the table, her head tilted up so he got to see those pretty green eyes. They were wide, panic in their depths, and it hurt his heart to know he was the cause.

But that was a hurt he'd endure, because she nodded and murmured, "Yes."

"Good," he said, standing and tossing a few bills on the table. "Come with me."

Then he took her hand and led her to the only place he knew could make her understand.

The cemetery.

# TWELVE

REBECCA

I t was a beautiful night for a graveside visit.

Perhaps that was a morbid thing to think, but with the full moon shining down on the graves, gilding them in silver while softening the hard edges of the grass and trees, everything was quiet and still.

But not relaxed.

Gabe was as un-relaxed as a person could get without saying anything. His jaw hard, shoulders stiff, spine straighter than a flag pole, to say nothing of his expression, which was icy.

He'd taken her hand, weaving their fingers together in a gentle grip, but with every step they took through the damp grass, he seemed to grow more rigid.

Then he stopped and her breath disappeared.

"Maggie," he murmured. "I want you to meet Rebecca."

She froze. "Gabe?"

He tugged her a little closer, so she was standing in front of the headstone and could read the inscription.

*Margaret Helen Jones, Beloved Fiancée and Friend*

"She didn't have any family except for me," he murmured, brushing some leaves from the granite and revealing the date she'd died on had been close to a decade before. "There was a group of us that were close in high school and college, but after Maggie died, it was . . . well, she'd been the glue. I was lost for a long time."

"How did she—?" She broke off, thinking it wasn't the most sensitive question to ask at a moment like this.

"Cancer."

Rebecca winced. "I'm so sorry."

"I loved her."

She touched his arm. "I can tell."

"We were supposed to get married."

Fuck. She'd known it, based on what he'd told her, what was written on the gravestone, but hearing the words out loud, the sadness embedded in those words. "I'm . . . *shit*, it sounds so cliché to just say sorry, but—"

"It was a tragedy," he murmured. "She was a wonderful soul." His eyes came to hers. "And why I stayed in medicine even after she was gone."

"You wanted to help people," Rebecca said.

"Yes. I got my degree, finished my residency, but couldn't stand working in a hospital setting."

"Did it remind you of her?"

He nodded. "Too much. I couldn't bear it, so when the opportunity came to work for the Gold, I jumped for it."

"How did that happen?"

"During my residency, I made friends with an orthopedic surgeon. We worked together a lot, and turned out I had a knack for hammering and screwing bones back together." He shrugged, a grin playing on the corners of his mouth. "His brother was a doctor with the group that worked for the Panthers. I stayed there for a few months, and he recommended me to the Gold when the opening came." Another shrug. "I got a lucky break."

"I know about lucky breaks," she murmured. "Mandy met me at a conference and recommended me to the leadership. I'd always dreamed I'd be working with elite athletes, but didn't think I'd make it this far. It's been really rewarding, though. The guys" —she laughed softly—"well, I was going to say they don't complain. But they do, of course. They just usually do what I advise *after* they finish complaining."

Gabe smiled. "That they do. So at this conference, did Mandy corner you and force you to do her bidding?"

Her smile mirrored his. "Basically."

"She's good at that."

Rebecca nodded. "That she is." A pause then gently, "I'm truly sorry about Maggie. It sounds like you were lucky to have had each other."

"Four months ago, I wouldn't have agreed with you." He led her to a bench tucked beneath an old tree. "Four months ago, I would have said it was the worst experience of my life, having her then losing her." He rotated to face her. "I loved her, but not in the way a man should love a woman. She was my best friend and I proposed because, yes, I loved her, but also because she was dying, because she would never be a doctor like she'd dream of. Because at least then I could give her one of her dreams."

"To get married?"

He nodded. "But in the end, I couldn't even give her that."

"So, you decided to be a doctor? To help people."

"I was already Pre-Med," he said. "So it wasn't totally altruistic. But yes, I knew very intimately what it would mean if I'd given up just because I was working eighty hours a week on little to no sleep."

"Just that?" Rebecca asked lightly and then because of everything he'd shared, and because it was impossible not to, she hugged him. "Oh, Gabe."

"I didn't tell you all that for sympathy," he said, wrapping his arms around her in return. "Though I'll take this hug all day, every day." He pulled back slightly and grinned down at her for a split second, after which his face returned to serious. "I told you because there was a reason I was a jerk. You look like her, Rebecca. On the outside—your hair is almost the exact shade of red, your eyes a similar color of green, but it's more than that," he added quickly when she sucked in a breath. "Because the biggest similarity is in here"—he touched her temple—"and here"—her heart —"You were both quiet, gentle souls. And yet, you both always sparked a fire within me."

Rebecca took a shaky breath, gently touched his cheek. "You can't say things like that."

"It's the truth," he murmured. "You're beautiful inside and out." His lips curved slightly. "Even if you do like cashew cheese."

She blinked back tears, forced a smile. "You like it, too."

"Maybe." His lips brushed her cheek.

"Also, you're uncommonly annoying."

He laughed, brushed his thumb across her lips. "And there's that spice I love so much."

"*Gabe*," she said on a shiver.

"I know," he murmured, eyes hot and making heat spiral in her center. "And here's me laying it all out there. I'm not asking for you to make a commitment, or for you to bind your soul with mine." He squeezed her hand. "All I'm asking is that we give ourselves the opportunity to explore the connection between us."

Her heart was pounding, terror mixed with longing. She wanted to run, to crawl back into her safe little shell, and she wanted to crawl into his lap and kiss him senseless.

But this was Gabe.

And he'd been honest with her, so she owed it to him to give the same in return.

Her words were shaky. "I don't know if I can be what you deserve."

"I'm just asking you to be you."

"*Gabe.*"

"That's it, sweetheart." He cupped her cheek. "I want you as you are."

Maybe it was what he shared, or perhaps it was that glorious Dr. Gabe Carter power again, or maybe, it was that for the first time in her life, she'd finally found the courage to go for something she wanted.

# Thirteen

## Gabe

"Absolutely not," Rebecca said a few days later, glaring up at him in the hall of the rink, arms crossed, cheeks flushed, eyes narrowed. "We are *not* having a pizza party in the middle of the playoff push—"

"The guys hit their goal," he reminded her, watching those pretty green irises spark fire. "They need a reward."

She tapped her foot, not quite a stomp but getting there, and he had to resist the urge to lean down and kiss her. "A reward is *not* salty meat products and greasy-phthalate-laced cheese."

"How about just a little of that salty meat?" He held up his thumb and forefinger, just the slightest bit apart.

"A little—" She gasped then seemed to realize he was teasing her.

*God, she's pretty,* he thought as her hands came up to grip his shoulders, jostling him lightly. She was just too fucking much, her mouth opening and closing in outrage. "You're—"

"Teasing," he supplied. "The phase two guys are going to wait for their next cheat day. And they promised me they'd go easy on the meat."

"You're—" She sputtered and even that was adorable. "You —" She huffed. "I can't believe you'd tease me about something like that—"

Unable to resist any longer, he bent and kissed her, cutting off her words, taking her into his arms, and not giving a damn they were in the hall, that anyone could walk by or pop their head out of their office and see them.

Which happened about two seconds after their lips touched.

The wolf-whistle made her jump, mouth jerking back.

"Yes!"

They both turned to see Mandy standing in the hall, fist raised mid-pump. Her husband, Blane, the perpetrator of said whistle, was behind her, a huge grin on his face.

"Carry on," Mandy said, taking her huge hockey player by the arm and dragging him back into the training suite, where no doubt the news of their kiss would be chugging right down that Gold gossip train.

"We've done it now," Rebecca said.

"I'm sorry." He touched her cheek. "I shouldn't have kissed you there."

"I'm guessing it won't be much of a surprise to anyone, considering how much time we've been spending together."

That was true. The team had been playing it cool for a long time, probably because Mandy understood they'd both needed time to get comfortable and had played mother hen.

The players did not fuck around when Mandy laid down the law.

"Yes, but—"

"Come with me," she said, and took his hand, leading him in the opposite direction of the locker and training rooms. They were in the bowels of the Gold Mine, the seventeen-thousand-plus seat arena that was the team's home rink above them. Noise was already beginning to filter down through the concrete, staff prepping the space for the fans that would soon enter.

But it would get louder.

There was absolutely nothing like hearing the collective cheers —or groans—from that many people at the same time. It hit Gabe in the gut every time, reverberating through his body, lighting his nerves on fire.

He wasn't even a player and it was beyond energizing.

Not realizing he'd stopped until she tugged his hand, he moved closer to Rebecca and matched her pace.

"Why are you the one freaking out," she mused, "when I'm the one with anxiety?"

Startled, he laughed.

"Just saying." She glanced up, brows raised.

This woman.

"Rebec—"

His words were cut off when she tugged him through the door that led to the ice and a blast of cold hit his face. He barely had time to react to the change in temperature before she yanked him again, this time in the direction of a black curtain. Two more steps and they were behind it.

"What—?"

She spun to face him, green eyes on fire, but before he could deduce what kind of fire it was—anger or desire—she rose on tiptoe and slanted her mouth across his.

*Ah.* Desire. Yeah, he could work with that.

Especially when he got soft lips, hot tongue, incredible breasts pressed against his chest.

Perhaps not the most intelligent thoughts, but they were all he could process as she wrapped her arms around his neck and kissed the living hell out of him. Thankfully, he managed to get his body to work, even if his brain was useless. He gripped her hips, lifting her up, bringing her mouth closer and her legs around his waist, and turning to press her against the wall.

Sweet. So fucking sweet.

He groaned when her legs tightened, hips tilting to rub against his cock, making sweat break out along his spine even in the cold arena.

Spice. Lots of hidden spice, exposed for him alone.

Yes, he was a possessive fucker. No, he didn't give a damn.

She nipped at his mouth, arching against him, holding him tighter, and he got the fuck out of his thoughts, focusing instead on kissing her back, on sweeping his tongue past her lips, on tasting every inch of her mouth while he still had air in his lungs.

Her hands clenched in his hair, pulling his head back as she sucked in gasping breaths, but Gabe didn't stop, *couldn't* stop, not when she was so close, smelled incredible, and was finally, *finally* in his arms.

He dipped, tracing his mouth across her jaw, down her throat, nipping the exposed skin just above her collarbone. She jerked and groaned, fingers in his hair clenching tighter, and he made a mental note for later that she liked it. But then she was tugging his head back up and their mouths collided as they kissed and kissed and *kissed*.

At least until the buzzer rang.

Then they both jumped apart, abruptly coming back into reality as they heard the noises around them—the arena filling up, the players jumping onto the ice for their pre-game skate, the crack of sticks and pucks—and Rebecca looked up at him, the guiltiest expression on her face.

"Whoops," she murmured.

He grinned and slowly let her feet hit the ground. "Best pre-game experience of my life," he said. "But I've got to get to work."

She nodded but bit her lip, eyes flickering with unease.

"Babe." Those pretty eyes came to him. "Thank you."

The uncertainty faded, pink staining the tops of her cheeks, even as a smile crept into the corners of her mouth. "You know what this means, right?"

"That you're stuck with me now?" he teased. "Or that the entire team is probably gossiping about us as we speak?"

"Yes," she said, pressing one more quick kiss to his lips before pulling back the curtain. "But it also means that you owe me a first date." Her hair flipped over her shoulder in a red wave as she glanced back at him and winked.

Winked.

His Rebecca.

He grinned.

"I think with the way you just kissed me, I might owe you ten dates."

She spun around in a movement so fast that he almost missed it. But he didn't miss the brush of her touch as she cupped his jaw briefly before continuing walking.

And he didn't miss her words.

"I'm going to hold you to that."

He grinned and trailed her down the hall, knowing that he absolutely could not wait to give her that first date.

———

As expected, Gabe endured an avalanche of shit-giving when he finally made it into the locker room, mostly because he'd been caught kissing Rebecca in the hall outside her office again when they'd returned from the ice. This time Max had stumbled onto them, and as the resident jokester—a title he'd given himself, not bequeathed by the team—Gabe had known his fate was sealed even before Max had made it back into the locker room.

Still, the guys had big hearts and though the quantity of shit shoveling in his direction was large, it wasn't mean.

They liked him.

They liked Rebecca.

They wanted them both to be happy.

Though Stefan, the Gold's captain, had given Gabe an eagle-eyed look when he'd made it into the room. Gabe knew that meant they would be having a "conversation"—yes, he said that mentally with air quotes—later because while Stefan was protective of all the Gold staff, the captain had a particular soft spot for the shy Rebecca, having told off more than a few of the guys when they'd complained about the diet or the awkward way she interacted with the players.

Stefan wouldn't be telling Gabe anything he didn't know.

In fact, after spending so much time together, he knew better than most how much Rebecca pushed through to live her life, and he wasn't going to jeopardize that. He'd witnessed her battling with herself, watched her expand against the barriers of her anxiety to go to new places, to be more comfortable in talking to people. Hell, it had been almost a full month before he'd begun seeing her eyes on a regular basis. Before that they were focused on spots over his shoulders, on her hands, the floor, anything but his own.

But she was strong and instead of drawing into herself, instead of allowing her world to shrink, she was trying to make it bigger.

And for that, she would always have his respect.

Not that she was always successful. There was a reason it had taken him four months to move from acquaintance to friend to . . . having ten dates. She'd canceled a lot in the beginning, and when they did make it out, their conversations weren't easy.

Eventually though, with patience on both their sides, they'd forged a friendship.

And lately, he'd sensed a change in her.

He'd felt those barriers begin to ease open.

So, no. He wasn't going to fuck this chance up with her. Not when every time that barrier peeled back a little further, he saw more of the wonderful woman he'd come to care so much about.

He checked in with Mandy in the training suite, made sure all the injured players had been seen and reevaluated as necessary by the physician team the Gold had partnered with. Gabe was technically an M.D., but his job description was Head Trainer. The team's physicians—including one onsite ER (emergency room) doctor, an orthopedist, and a PCP (primary care physician) were required to be provided by the Gold for each of the home games —but they also had a team of specialists that worked together with Gabe and the rest of the training staff to keep the team healthy.

He could have given up his job as trainer, joined the practice treating the team, but that meant he wouldn't technically be an employee of the Gold, nor be able to travel with the team.

Gabe didn't want to work with the team only during particular times. He wanted to be an important member of the organization.

Plus, his training and experience working under the team for the Panthers meant that he'd lived that reality long enough to know he hadn't wanted it permanently. Luckily, the management of the Gold had seen his additional degree as a bonus.

And it was true. He and Mandy both were M.D.'s, and while that didn't cross over perfectly with everything a trainer did on a day-to-day basis, it gave them the experience and vernacular to work more closely with the physician team. So, it was a win-win. He got to be a full-fledged member of the Gold staff and was also able to put his special skills to use.

Coop was in the training suite when Gabe came in, not dressed for the game after failing the concussion protocol two nights before. He'd taken a big hit, came off rattled, and that meant he'd needed time to recover.

Both the physician and the training team agreed on this.

Coop did not.

"I'm fine," he grumbled to Mandy as she surveyed another strike against him—a large bruise on his ribs.

"I'll say this once more and then I'm not going to be held responsible for my actions if you continue your complaining. You have *one* brain. One!" Coop huffed out a sigh, and she held up a roll of tape in response. "Remember, I can use this in all sorts of uncomfortable places if you keep annoying me."

Gabe leaned one hip against the table Coop was lying on.

They both glanced at him, Coop's lips curving slightly. "You hear that she's threatening me?"

Gabe put out his hand and Mandy tossed him the roll. "If you think she's bad . . . just consider what the two of us can do if we put our minds together."

Coop's mouth pressed flat. "You guys suck."

"One brain," Mandy reminded him then sighed. "Dammit. I said I was going to only say it once more. That's twice now."

"Parenting rots your brain," Gabe said.

"Parenting is the best thing I've ever done."

Coop grinned. "That's what my mom used to say."

"Used?" Gabe asked, knowing full well Coop's mom was alive. She'd brought in a pan of mac n cheese for the team just the previous week when she'd been visiting her son. Luckily, it had fallen on a cheat day or Rebecca might have stabbed Coop and the other phase two players for daring to eat it, thus revealing some of that spice to the boys on the team.

They couldn't have that.

The spice was Gabe's.

"Yeah," Coop said. "She *used* to say it." A beat. "Before I got old enough to give her gray hairs."

Mandy flicked her own ponytail over her shoulder, seemingly checking it for the gray buggers. "When was that?"

"The moment I was conceived." Coop grinned.

Gabe snorted and Mandy smacked him lightly. "Don't encourage him," she muttered, shaking her head as she began spreading her special bruise cream on Coop's ribs.

"Who?" Coop asked.

"*Either* of you." She placed a heating pad on his ribs, pointed between the two of them. "Neither of you encourage the other."

"Too late." Gabe grinned and fist-bumped Coop, before waving goodbye to Mandy and promising to catch up with her after the game to go over any outstanding injuries or treatment plans.

Then he slipped on his jacket, grabbed his bag, and hightailed it to the bench.

It was time to watch some hockey.

# Fourteen

S he surveyed the contents of her closet and sighed.

It had been two days since her make-out session with Gabe, two busy days, more on his part than hers, since her job had leveled out at this point in the season, but his was ramping up.

Playoffs were close.

The Gold were second in the Western Conference and only a few points back from first, which meant they were in good shape.

But that was more from a scoreboard perspective.

The injuries were piling up.

Which meant that Gabe and Mandy were working overtime trying to keep the boys healthy.

Brit's shoulder was acting up. Coop had just been cleared from the concussion protocol that morning, but his ribs weren't a hundred percent. Max had broken a finger. Stefan had taken a puck in the face in the game two nights before and had needed twenty-something stitches. Blue was rehabbing a sprained knee, and Blane . . . well, Blane was one of only a few players she could think of who were currently uninjured.

The season was long, consisting of eighty-two highly physical, sometimes brutal games, and she admired the mental fortitude and athletic stamina it took for the guys to make it through.

She couldn't do it, couldn't imagine anyone *wanting* to, but she admired them all the same.

What she *didn't* admire was the lack of anything worthy enough for a first date with Gabe in her closet. He would be over in less than an hour, and she had . . . absolutely nothing.

They'd been out together dozens of times over the last few months, but this was different.

This was not as friends.

This was as more.

With expectations and anticipation and . . . she had nothing.

Her pulse began pounding, tightening her throat, making her dizzy enough that she had to sink to the floor and drop her head to her knees.

She couldn't do this. She *couldn't*.

She wanted it so bad and yet, she just couldn't. *Couldn't. Couldn't. Couldn't.*

Groaning, Rebecca leaned back against her bed, dropping her head back to the mattress and trying to stop the cycle in her brain. She didn't want to be like this. Yes, she'd come to terms with the fact that she wasn't broken, but dammit, this extra burden she carried felt god awful and heavy at times.

Especially when she just wanted to be a girl who was excited about a first date, rather than one with anxiety that had been triggered because she was doing something new with someone important and was terrified she'd blow it.

She picked up her phone, typed out a message, and miserably hit send.

*I don't think I can do this.*

The text went through, and she dropped her head back to her knees. Barely thirty seconds passed before her cell buzzed. Sucking in a deep breath, she picked it up and looked at the screen.

Gabe had responded.

*Funny you said that, because I sent you something.*

She frowned, waiting for another text to come through to explain the cryptic message. But none did.

*Sent what?*

This time she didn't get a chance to read any reply that might have come through because there was a knock at her door. She glanced down at herself, ensuring that she bore some semblance of clothing—a bathrobe with ratty sweats counted, she decided— then hurried to the door. Part of her hoped Gabe was the thing he'd sent her. The rest was worried. She'd wanted to make an effort tonight, for him to see her together and looking beautiful.

Not in holey clothes and spiraling.

Another knock came when she was a few feet away from the door.

"Coming!" she called and then glanced through the peephole.

And froze. *Oh God.*

"No use hiding," Bex called through the door, Mandy and Sara behind her. Their arms were full of bags. Clothing bags. And one that looked like makeup.

Oh. God. Nope. No way. She couldn't—

"I brought wine!" Brit said, and Rebecca watched the tall, slender goalie of the Gold slip in front of the other girls. "Gabe said it was your favorite brand."

Damn that man.

"It's a cheat day," Brit continued. "Please, don't make me drink all three bottles by myself."

"Th-three?" she said on a gasp and reached for the lock, pulling the door open. "Brit! You can't drink three bottles by yourself, th-that's not on the diet plan. Your pH levels would be—"

"As if we would let her," Bex said, nudging Rebecca out of the way and pushing the door wide. "Oh lord," she said, eyes trailing her from head to toes. "We've got work to do. Come on, ladies."

She barreled into the apartment, walking straight over to the kitchen and opening cabinets until she found the one with wine glasses. As she pulled six out, lining them up on the counter, Brit slipped by, holding up the bottles as though they were a key. And maybe they were, Rebecca thought, but didn't have long to focus on that because then Mandy touched her arm.

"Is this okay?" her friend asked.

"It's—" Not okay exactly, but it also *wasn't* not okay. Which didn't make any sense in the least. but all she knew was that two minutes before she'd been freaking out about not having anything to wear and now she had friends on her doorstep.

Because of Gabe.

She sniffed, eyes stinging. "You don't have to help—"

"Shh." Mandy hugged her. "It's okay," her friend said. "We *want* to be here. But we're also a rowdy bunch. So, give me the high sign if it becomes too much."

It was too much already.

And yet, it was also perfect.

"Thanks for coming," she said.

"We'll keep barreling into your life until you kick us out," Bex declared. "I've taken a page out of Kevin's book. Just be sweet and persistent until the other person gives."

"You can be sweet?" Brit teased.

Bex waggled her brows. "What do you think? Kev—"

"Ew," Sara said, the final body making her way through the door. The former figure skater was soft-spoken but had been through hell and had a spine of steel. It was one of those things that infuriated Rebecca about herself. She had no trauma in her life. For sure, her parents divorcing hadn't been easy, especially when her dad had taken off and built a new family afterward and her mom had shut down to the point of negligence.

But kids went through that all the time.

One parent left. The other wasn't great.

They coped.

Hell, her sister had the same circumstances and it hadn't slowed her down in the least. She'd just straightened her shoulders and finished college, getting a job at Fortune 500 company and making her way through the ranks there.

Now Sandra was on her own, bringing bigger and bigger clients in to her consulting firm without missing a beat.

And Rebecca had a blog.

Yes, she was also with the Gold.

But it wasn't Wall Street or Fortune 500, and so it couldn't begin to compare. At least according to Sandra and her father.

"You okay?" Sara, the former gold medalist turned artist, asked, pulling her out of her own thoughts.

"I don't know if okay is the right word," Rebecca admitted. "But thank you for coming. I feel like such a dummy saying this aloud, but I don't have anything to wear."

"Not dumb," Sara said. "This is important. You want to mark the moment."

Yes, she did.

Also, there went her stomach again, fluttering and tightening and—

"Wine!" Bex declared, shoving a glass under Rebecca's nose and handing out the rest of the filled goblets.

"Who's the last one for?" Rebecca asked.

"Me."

She turned, saw Calle standing in the doorway.

"Hi." Calle waved awkwardly. "Is it okay if I invade? I don't really know a lot of people in town, and Brit mentioned—"

Rebecca's heart skipped a beat, though for the first time in a long time it wasn't with regards to herself. Calle was uncomfortable. Rebecca could make that better, make it easier.

Wow.

Could it sometimes be just that simple?

Not a cure, not a be-all-end-all.

But perhaps a way to cope.

Tucking that thought away to deal with later, she took Calle's hand and tugged her into the apartment, closing the door behind them. "Come in," she said belatedly and smiled at herself before plunking the glass into Calle's fingers. "I'm having a closet crisis, and I'm hoping that all these bags that Bex hauled in mean you guys are going to bail me out."

Bex grinned and handed her the final goblet. "Bail you out how? Do we have carte blanche—?"

"I would highly advise against that," Brit said.

"But Rebecca—*Bex* dresses so well," Sara pointed out.

"If Rebecca wanted to look like a high-powered attorney for her first date with Gabe, then yes," Brit said. "But I'm guessing she doesn't want to go that route."

"Rebecca should feel comfortable in what she wears," Mandy pointed out.

"I know fashion, and—"

Brit rolled her eyes. "You two may have the same name, but that doesn't mean—"

"But just saying," Calle said, carefully maneuvering into the fray. "I don't know if the robe/sweats combo is the way to go."

Sara snorted.

Rebecca laughed. She'd witnessed Brit and Bex going around and around more than once, and while tonight it was happening in *her* apartment over what *she* was going to wear on her date, she didn't feel uncomfortable. Instead, it just felt like she was at work, with her people. And that made it okay. "When Gabe said he sent me something, I didn't think he meant a bickering makeover squad."

"How about a bickering makeover squad with presents?" Bex asked, not missing a beat.

"That's better," Rebecca agreed.

"Okay. Wine. Then closet survey. Then bag appraisal. Deal?" Bex asked, or rather pronounced to the group at large.

"Deal," Rebecca said and took a sip from her glass. And as everyone followed suit, she led them into her bedroom.

An hour and all three bottles of wine later, she'd texted Gabe and put him off by another thirty minutes.

Sara was doing her hair and makeup, thanks to her former

figure skater roots, and Bex had put together an outfit Rebecca would never have dreamed of. Mixing a clingy tank covered by a favorite lace vest Mandy had found in Rebecca's closet with a tight pair of pleather pants Bex had pulled out of one of the bags. Calle and Brit had mostly stood back and watched, drinking wine, but they *had* chosen her necklace, and the long, draping chains of silver and gold went perfectly with the entire look.

It was the sexiest she'd ever felt.

It was also the most time she'd spent with other women since middle school.

She hadn't realized how much she'd been missing that, connecting with women, being around a gabbing group of women, and *participating* in that conversation rather than restricting herself to the outside because she felt awkward. That wasn't to say it had all gone completely smooth. She'd stumbled over her words a few times and had gotten really quiet when Bex had pulled out a matching black lace and panty set, but no one had made a big deal of it. Well, they'd chastised Bex about her forwardness while reminding her of the fact that this was only a first date. To which she'd responded that Rebecca and Gabe had had four months of foreplay—*accurate*—and plus, there was nothing wrong with a woman having sex on the first date if that's what she wanted—*also true.*

But the point was, even when things didn't go perfectly smooth and everyone wasn't in complete agreement, they still continued moving forward.

Plus, they all had their own awkward moments.

The difference was that while there was good-natured teasing in response, no one made anyone else feel bad.

Lifting up rather than slamming down.

She hadn't recognized it before.

"Gabe texted!" Mandy called, tone bordering on a shriek. "He's coming in ten minutes whether we're ready or not."

Rebecca jerked and nearly impaled herself with the mascara wand.

Sara put a hand on her shoulder. "Freeze. I'm almost done."

Bex was scurrying around the room, grabbing clothes and shoving them into bags. Calle gathered wine glasses. Brit and Mandy began straightening the mess in Rebecca's closet.

"It's okay," she began. "I can—"

"Hush," Sara said. "Let us do this for you, okay?"

Instead of arguing—or nodding since that mascara wand was still very close to her eye—she just whispered, "Okay."

Two minutes later she was done, and Sara was packing up the makeup bag, which she set on Rebecca's bathroom counter and wouldn't hear any argument about Rebecca paying for any of it. Five minutes after that, her heels were on, her closet was straightened, the wine glasses were drying on the rack, and the girls were walking out the door.

She opened her mouth to thank them again.

"Absolutely not," Brit said, hugging her briefly before leaving.

"Put that thanks away," Sara chimed in.

"But—"

"I got to use you as my real-life Barbie doll, so shush."

"Exactly," Bex said then grinned. "Plus, we'll be watching Gabe's reaction from the bushes." She held up her camera.

Which Calle promptly snatched from her hand. "Um. Nope, we will not be watching from the bushes," she said and started walking, Bex hurrying after her, demanding the camera back. "Thanks for letting me hang out!" she called before descending the stairs.

"I'd better go make sure that doesn't turn into something," Mandy said.

"Calle *is* strong."

Mandy smirked. "And Bex fights dirty."

Rebecca laughed then hugged her tight. "I know I haven't been an easy person to be friends with, but—"

"Shut up before you make me smack you," Mandy declared fiercely. "You're smart, beautiful, and loyal. I've never seen you not do the right thing, even if it's hard. Yes, you're quiet and reserved, and maybe you struggle to put yourself out there, but you're perfect the way you are, Rebecca." A beat. "It's easy to like you. To *love* you. No matter who told you differently." She pulled back, jostled her lightly. "Even if that person was you."

Then as if she hadn't just dropped an atomic bomb on her soul, Mandy left.

But she stopped at the top of the stairs.

"Also, you're as good for Gabe as he is for you," she said. "He's taken the blinders off. Because of you." Mandy hesitated for a second longer before descending. "All *you*, Rebecca."

Sucking in a breath as her friends disappeared, she carefully closed the door to her apartment, teetering on her heels, mind swirling.

But this time it was for a different reason.

This time it was a *good* swirling.

Something she'd never thought was possible until the tornado of girls had invaded her apartment and her life.

At Gabe's direction.

She smiled and went to retrieve her purse. Her legs were shaking and her heart was pounding, but that wouldn't stop her.

# FIFTEEN

GABE

He was going to kill Mandy and company.

Not really, of course, but they'd taken the sweet veneer of Rebecca completely away and now she was all spice, and he was going to have a perpetual case of blue balls.

Hence, the killing.

But then his gaze made it back to her face and he saw.

Scratch that, he was going to buy them each a case of wine. Joy radiated inside her, shining through her eyes and punching him in the gut. *Fuck.* That might have been the purest thing he'd seen since . . . well, Maggie. He'd watched her radiate joy when she'd gotten her acceptance to medical school, when she'd been declared cancer-free the first time in high school, when he'd visited her while she was sick.

Gabe swallowed hard.

"What is it?" Rebecca cupped his cheek lightly. "Are you all right?"

"I feel so lucky to have a woman like you in my life."

Her breath caught.

"You're beautiful." He touched her cheek.

She smiled. "You wouldn't have thought that ninety minutes ago when I was freaking out and wearing holey sweats and a ratty bathrobe."

"I meant on the inside."

"Gabe!"

He blinked at her tone. "What?"

"Don't make me cry! Sara did my makeup, and Bex and Mandy helped me with my clothes, and Brit and Calle picked out my necklace—" She sniffed. "And now you're being so unbelievable you're going to make me cry."

It was punctuating the statement with a stomp of her foot that did it.

He grabbed her by the waist and hauled her close. There was just enough time for her to say, "My lipstick!" and for him to growl, "I don't give a fuck," before he slammed his mouth down onto hers.

Thankfully, she forgot about the lipstick and was right there with him.

Her hands came up to his head, weaving into his hair, and she launched herself into his arms, those gorgeous long legs wrapping around his hips.

"Fuck, yes," he murmured against her lips.

She moaned in response, her tongue slipping into his mouth to tangle with his. Heat burst down his spine, and he knew if he didn't stop them in the next few moments, they would keep going all night.

Gabe wanted that. *Fuck*, he wanted it.

But she deserved a first date.

He pulled away, albeit slowly, their lips almost reluctant to part. Her little mewl of disappointment nearly undid the infinitesimal control he'd regained, but in the end, he did manage to slowly lower her feet to the floor.

"I love how you end up in my arms every time we kiss, sweetheart."

Her lips were swollen, her cheeks flushed, but she didn't back down. "Don't try to say you didn't like it."

"That's not in question," he said. "The problem is that I liked it so much we might miss our dinner reservations."

She grinned, the stink.

"Those pants should be illegal, you look so fucking good." Pink spreading on her cheeks as he took a step back, hands clenching at his sides so he didn't grab her again. "Do you have everything you need?"

"Let me grab my coat."

"I can keep you warm."

She froze, then saw he was joking . . . kind of.

"I think that's what got us into this problem in the first place," she teased.

"Maybe."

Her fingers clenched on the doorframe. "I'd say come in but—"

"*That's* really what got us into the problem in the first place," he said.

"Exactly." With a grin, she disappeared into her apartment, reappearing a few seconds later with her coat. "Okay, *now* I'm ready."

Gabe helped her into it then slid an arm around her waist. "Ready for the most awesomest first date in the history of all first dates?"

"I'm ready to be with you," she said. "Whatever form that takes."

Yeah. If he hadn't spent the last four months falling in love with this woman, that right there would have done it.

———

Little Italy.

Not the place most well-known for vegan menus.

Gabe figured most restaurants had bought stock in meat,

cheese, and cream, but there was a small hole in the wall that offered up two menus. One for normal people, like him, he'd teased, and one for the crazy vegans.

Rebecca had laughed when he'd told her that, the sound gliding along the inside of his heart, making him think sappy thoughts as the light tinkling noise tapped on the inside of organs and filled him with joy.

Dinner had been easy, and hands down, the best meal of his life. But now he had to say goodnight to the woman he'd come to love.

And he didn't want to.

Now, instead of poetry, cue the petulant little child inside him.

They crested the top of the stairs and his heart sank.

Yes, he was whipped. No, he'd decided that wasn't a bad thing. Especially when he could smell the delicate scent of the rose he'd bought for her from the woman who'd come over to the table during dinner. Rebecca had picked the one with the broken stem, the one the lady selling them had tried to say was garbage, and tucked it behind one ear. That floral perfume had been teasing him the entire drive home, mixing with her cinnamon scent, and right about then, he wanted to roll around in it.

Lie. He wanted to roll around with *her*.

But that wasn't going to happen.

Well, not tonight anyway.

Because . . . why was that again exactly?

He racked his brain as they walked to her door, trying to remember all the reasons that he had to go home to his place and not talk his way into hers. He'd started the evening with several and was now drawing a blank.

She slipped her purse from her shoulder, retrieving her keys from the depths when he remembered.

Respect.

That's right.

What an idiot he was.

Rebecca unlocked her door, pushed it wide.

"Well, goodni—"

She grabbed his shirt by the lapels and yanked him inside, slamming the door shut the same moment she slammed her mouth down onto his.

"Four months," she said, tugging at the buttons of his shirt. "Don't try to get noble on me now."

"Rebecca—" She nipped at his chin. "Baby—" His jaw. "We should—" *Plink. Plink.* Buttons on his shirt flew.

"Stop thinking so hard," she said, stepping back and reaching for the zipper of her jacket. She tugged it down sharply. "And fuck me."

His cock had been hard from the moment her mouth had touched his. Her words turned it to granite. Her coat and vest dropping to the floor turning it to . . . diamond—or something appropriately hard.

Her shirt following suit had him obeying her order to stop thinking.

Black lace. Ivory skin.

Hot emerald eyes. A flush drifting down her throat, caressing the skin of her breasts.

She reached for the button of her pants.

He moved, sweeping her up into his arms, opening his mouth to ask if she was sure—

"My bedroom," she interrupted and then her lips met his and he was walking, her mouth on his making his head spin.

Or perhaps that was her hand.

Because those fingers had slipped beneath the hem of his T-shirt to stroke his stomach. But they didn't stay there. Rather, they slipped beneath the waistband of his pants and cupped him over his boxer briefs.

Then under.

That was the moment he finally stopped thinking.

# Sixteen

## Rebecca

Her thoughts were mid-swirl.

But instead of panic, she felt need and desire and a lot of *more. Faster. Now.*

Gabe dropped her on the bed, rearing back to tug off her heels, before returning to slant his mouth across hers. His hands moved in tandem, one coming up to cup her face, angling it so he could kiss her deeper while the other moved up and down her side, trailing low enough to tease the skin just under the waist-band of her pants and then back up, along her side, her ribs, the outside of her breast.

She shivered but set her own fingers to work on the remaining buttons of his shirt, wanting, *needing* to feel his naked skin against hers.

Thankfully, he seemed to want that, too, because he sat up and yanked the shirt over his head without bothering with the rest of the buttons then was back on top of her, lips descending.

Rebecca stopped him. "Wait," she gasped.

Gabe blinked, the haze of desire replaced by concern. "Did I hurt—?"

She pushed up onto one elbow, used her free hand to cup his jaw. "No," she murmured. "I wanted to do this." Leaning back, she arched enough to slip her hands under her shoulders and unhooked her bra. A quick shimmy later, it was on the floor.

The garbled sound he made was totally worth the sliver of insecurity she felt lying there spread out beneath him, upper half fully on display.

Well, that and the heat in his eyes.

And the way his hands shook.

Because, in an instant, the embarrassment was gone, replaced by need and desire and an impossible to resist urge to put her hands on him again.

So she did.

She traced her fingers along the curves of his shoulders, down his chest, cupping his pecs and brushing through the light dusting of dark hair covering them. His breath caught when she traced over one nipple, then the other, stomach clenching to reveal squares of muscles as they trailed lower.

"I haven't done this a lot," she admitted, tracing them over the waistband of his slacks, dipping a fingertip beneath to feel the hot skin below.

Gabe hissed out a breath. "You're tormenting me just fine."

She laughed, wrapped her arms around his middle, and tugged him down lightly. He followed her lead, coming closer, giving her what she wanted—which was to lean his weight more fully on top of her. That heat, that comforting pressure was exactly what she needed.

"I've been with two people," she said. "Once in high school, which as you might imagine, wasn't great since neither of us knew what the hell we were doing. But eventually we figured out a few things."

He flicked his tongue over her earlobe, making her shiver. "Babe, you don't have to—"

"The second was after things got bad with me. A total disaster." She turned her head to meet his eyes. "I couldn't relax. He couldn't read me. I wasn't confident enough to tell him when something wasn't working." She sucked in a breath, forced her racing heart to calm. "You're not a fan of jackhammer sex, are you?" Heat flooded her cheeks, part of her unable to believe she'd just said that aloud, while the rest of her knew that she could say it because it was *Gabe* in her bed.

Gabe who'd spent four months being her friend.

Gabe who was funny, kind, and sweet.

Gabe who could kiss like sin.

In that moment, however, he grinned down at her. "Is that what you want?"

She shook her head quickly. "God, no."

He laughed. "I happen to do non-jackhammer sex really well." A beat. "If you'd stop talking long enough for me to do so."

"Got it," she said and started to reach for him before pausing. "I have condoms in my nightstand. I'm not on the pill, and—"

He pulled his wallet from his back pocket, extracted a condom from inside. "Freshly put there tonight." He flipped it to show her the date on the back. "Even expires in two whole years."

"I thought you were going to have us wait."

"I like to be prepared."

She laughed.

"So, can I get back to kissing you now?" he asked lightly. "Or would you like me to discuss my sexual partners as well?"

Rebecca shuddered. "God, no. But Gabe—" She broke off, not sure how to word what she wanted to say. She was comfortable now, body raring to go and her mind right alongside it, urging her to jump in and stop thinking. But what if that changed? What if she *couldn't*?

"If it's too much, we stop," he said gently, reminding her again how much he'd come to understand her over the last four months. "It's only complicated if we make it that way. You want me, right?"

She nodded.

His hips pressed lightly against hers, the hard length of his cock making her gasp and thrust back. "It's clear I want you," he said. "That *you* want me. So we explore that however far we want tonight."

"You make it sound easy."

His brows waggled. "*I'm* easy." She giggled and he nuzzled her throat, whispering in her ear. "I just want you, baby. However, you're comfortable."

She bit her lip.

"Okay?"

"Okay," she said and hesitated.

Gabe, of course, read her hesitation. "What is it?"

She took a deep breath, pushed away the fear and asked for what she wanted. "Do you think you can kiss me again?" He grinned, lips coming toward hers, but she arched up and placed a hand on her breast. "Here."

Heat in those gorgeous espresso eyes, that grin going liquid and sending desire spiraling outward from her middle.

"I can do that," he murmured. "In a minute." His mouth dropped to hers.

His tongue could do absolutely wicked things, but she liked his particular brand of wicked and managed to meet him stroke for stroke. At least until his hand cupped her breast, caressing it gently then slightly harder when she pressed it up into his palm, his thumb shifting to tease the tight bud of her nipple.

She groaned, ripping her mouth from his, and he took the opportunity to kiss his way down her throat, along her collarbone, and into the space between her breasts. His jaw was roughened with stubble and the prickly sensation raised goose bumps on her skin. But even as she was still shivering, he took advantage of her distraction and sucked one nipple deeply into his mouth.

Okay, really, that was to *her* advantage.

She arched up, gripping the back of his head to hold him in place, moisture flooding between her thighs, only loosening her grip slightly when he made it clear he was trying to give the same enthusiastic attention to her other breast.

"Fuck, Gabe," she moaned.

He laved his tongue over the sensitive tip, bit lightly, the other fingers of his hand sliding down to the button on her pants. With one flicking movement, he had it open and was slipping his hand beneath the waistband.

She was soaked, absolutely drenched, and he groaned when his fingertips hit that wet, hot space between her thighs.

Not that she wasn't right there with him, legs automatically trying to widen, hips tilting up to prolong the contact. Unfortunately, the tight pants Gabe had been admiring all night meant that she didn't get very far.

"Here." He extracted his hand, gripped the waistband and tried to tug them down.

And got all of six inches before they bunched and tangled at her hips.

The pleather stuck and twisted, the fabric catching on her sweaty skin, and they spent several minutes straining, yanking, and cursing before they managed to pull them off her ankles.

Her underwear came off with them, but Rebecca wasn't complaining, not after their struggle for dominance with black faux-leather.

Tossing them aside, Gabe stole her mouth in a kiss that sent her pulse skyrocketing, breaking away only long enough to say, "I can't decide if I love or hate those pants."

"Love on," she gasped as he bent and sucked her nipple into his mouth again. "Hate the process of taking them off."

"Mmm," he agreed, fingers trailing down, dipping back between her thighs. His mouth spent some quality time with her other breast before trailing down her stomach and replacing his fingers. Or rather, working in tandem with his fingers, which were spreading her wide, while his lips descended onto her clit.

That was nice, as was the way his tongue flicked out, but it wasn't until he sucked the bundle of nerves deep that she was gasping and writhing, lights flashing behind her eyes and her hips jerking.

"*Oh God,*" she groaned when he nipped, and pleasure exploded through her body. Every nerve stood up in rigid attention, heat building in her center, filling her up, burning, growing, spreading until finally it burst and she was reduced to ash.

She couldn't see, couldn't hear. Could only feel pure pleasure burning through her.

All that remained were embers. Her soul was in tatters, her skin only cinder.

Until she floated back to Earth with Gabe cradling her close. Then she was reborn, a phoenix from the ashes.

"Hi," he murmured.

"Hi," she sighed inanely.

"Okay?"

She nodded. "I wasn't sure I was even in this universe for most of that."

"I hope that's a good thing."

A grin. "It's the best thing. The best thing I've ever."

His smile matched hers, but he didn't move, didn't make any indication that he was going to take it further. She smiled into his shoulder. That was so Gabe. And that meant *she* needed to be the one to say it was okay.

It was funny. That should have created pressure, her having to be the one who set the boundaries, the one who pushed them. But instead of pressure, she felt relaxed, comfortable, *relieved.* Not a lot tended to happen on her terms, and him giving her that gift —one of patience and understanding—made it easier for her to peek out from behind her armor.

Which was why the moment she could lift her arm, she raised it in the direction of the nightstand and the condom he'd put there earlier.

"Are you—?"

She tore it open with her teeth, extracted the latex circle, and rolled it down his length.

Gabe didn't ask if she was sure this time, didn't stop her, or put on the condom himself. Instead, he watched her with hot brown eyes as she stroked it down his cock, slowly protecting them both.

And when she lay back and spread her legs, he moved on top of her, bracing himself on one elbow while lacing the fingers of his other hand through hers.

"Okay?"

She lifted one leg, wrapped it around his hip. "Okay."

He slid home slowly, both of them wanting to savor the moment. She'd never felt anything quite like it, and definitely not when she'd been with other people in the past. This . . . connection with Gabe couldn't compare to those experiences in the least. It was more and it was everything. It was being close to someone, in ways she never could have imagined.

It was the most intense interaction of her life.

And yet, it wasn't overwhelming or too much. She didn't feel the need to withdraw or hide behind her shy. She wanted to move out further, to throw every part of herself at him, knowing he wouldn't fail to catch a single piece.

Then he moved.

Her focus shifted, concentrating on the way he felt, how big and hard he was, how deep he was thrusting, how he adjusted his angle as he kissed her, driving her pleasure back up so she was spiraling tighter and tighter just as he was.

She tore her mouth away, gasping in air as she got near the edge, not quite there, not sure what was missing, just knowing that she was so damned close.

But he understood what she needed, unlacing their hands and slipping his thumb between her thighs to press firmly down on her clit. It was almost too much, that pressure, riding that fine line between great and overwhelming.

In the end, it was just right.

She shot over the edge.

Gabe thrust once, twice more before falling alongside her.

But even as pleasure grabbed him, he still held her as though she were the most precious object in his world.

And for that moment, she believed it was true.

————

"Shh," she said, later that evening after they'd gone out for a midnight snack of freeze-dried snap peas and wine—remarkably, they paired well together. Now they'd just finished the new episodes of *Love is Blind* and were chatting. Naked.

That was a new twist to their consumption of wine and reality television.

But it was also a great one. And it compelled her to confide in him.

"How am I supposed to listen when we just got finished watching Barnett treat the women that way?"

"He's the villain for now," she said with a shrug. "And also a bit of a tool bag. But just wait until you see what Jessica does."

"I can't believe you watched ahead," he huffed. "It's an outrage."

She lightly bit his shoulder. "I'm trying to tell you something important here."

"What, baby?" he asked, reality TV paused as he realized she was serious. "Are you okay with tonight? With everything that happened?"

Her heart squeezed. This man. "Yes," she said, touching his cheek. "I'm fine but—" She sucked in a breath. "Look, you know I struggle with anxiety, but while I wasn't an easy-going kid—I definitely didn't roll with the punches well—I wasn't always like I've been over the last ten years."

He tensed. "What happened?"

"My dad left." She shrugged. "It was a long time coming. My mom was like me, but worse. She refused to get help and things . . . got worse over time. I don't blame him, exactly, especially because he was the one who got me to a therapist, who paid for it without question."

"Why do I feel like there's a *but* coming?"

Her head dropped back to the pillow. "Because there is. He didn't understand it. Even after twenty years with my mom struggling, he didn't get that it wasn't something you just got better from."

"He wanted a cure."

"Yes."

"And there isn't one."

She pressed her lips together. "No," she said. "There are techniques I can use to push through, ways that some of it gets easier, but no, it's always there. Even when I lock it away, that anxiety is struggling against that box."

"It's part of you."

A nod. "I'm not going to be cured and someday feel totally fine small-talking with strangers or getting up in front of everyone to address a crowd. New places are always going to be a challenge. I'll always need to research and—"

"I don't care."

"You say that now."

"No." His voice was firm. "I say that after spending almost every day with you for the last four months. I say that after watching you struggle and seeing you push through things that make you uncomfortable. I say that after having you cancel plans and Yelp like no one's business." He picked up her hand, laced their fingers together. "But I also say that after you forgave me for being a jerk, after you didn't hold it against me *one fucking time*."

"It wasn't your fault—"

"It *was*," he said, cupping her cheek with his free hand, voice intense. "You know what made me come after you that day? What made me want to be friends, even while thinking that I should stay far, far away from anyone who reminded me of Maggie and the pain that came from loving her?"

She shook her head.

"*You*. I saw fire in your eyes when you told me off. And then I watched that spark disappear. Because of me." He sucked in a breath, released it slowly. "I knew if I loved Maggie at all—even as just a friend, definitely as desperate for it to be more than that so she could have what she deserved—then I needed to find a way to make your fire come back and to make sure it never disappeared again." A beat. "Because I knew the universe had sent me a gift. A second chance. But this time, it sent me one I could love as desperately as she deserved."

Her lungs froze.

He touched her nose, said lightly, "In case you're wondering, the gift was you."

She sucked in a breath, every bit of relaxed feeling that had been inside her faded. Because he'd raised the stakes. This wasn't just boyfriend-girlfriend. This was more, more *important*.

More risk.

And he kept talking, for once not recognizing that it was too much, that she needed to catch her breath and process. "You took my blinders off, sweetheart. You showed me you, and I wasn't going to squander it, even if that meant I spent the rest of my life as only your friend."

"Gabe." Her heart pounded, her head spun.

"I love you."

No. *No.*

This was—

She couldn't—

Every fear she'd locked down exploded out of that box in her mind. He couldn't begin to understand. This was exactly what she was afraid would happen. He didn't know what it would be like. It would start off great, like with her parents, but it would sour. Of course, it would. She was too much work and stress. He deserved—

Sweat broke out along her spine, her mouth worked frantically, trying to find words, *any word* that might stop—

"Baby," he said gently, but his eyes were worried. He'd realized that she was too far gone.

But it was too late.

"*No.*" She shoved him back, slipped from beneath the covers and ran into the bathroom, slamming and locking the door behind her.

He had to go.

He *had* to.

She closed her eyes and rested her head on her knees.

This couldn't be.

It was never going to work.

# SEVENTEEN

GABE

He'd fucked up.
He'd missed the signs.
He—
"Fuck," he muttered, staring at the closed door of the bathroom and wondering how he was going to fix this.

Too much too fast, after he'd spent the last four months playing the long game.

Moron.

She'd been trying to share something important with him, and he'd talked all over it, had missed it was too much. So much for taking the blinders off.

Carefully, he eased out of bed and slipped on his boxer briefs then crossed over to the bathroom door and knocked lightly.

No answer.

Not that he'd really expected there to be.

But the question was, did he push, or did he give her space?

Every instinct told him he couldn't let her be alone in the bathroom, allowing whatever terrible thoughts were swirling in her head to fester, but . . . he'd already pushed her past her boundaries once, and look where that had gotten them.

He started to turn away, to pace the length of the bedroom as he processed, but then he heard it.

The sniffle.

The memory of her voice in his mind. *I'm not broken.*

And he knew. She deserved for him to react in the same way he would if she didn't have anxiety. She deserved for him to give a shit that she was crying by herself on the bathroom floor.

She deserved to not be alone.

So he crossed back to the door and tried the handle.

Locked.

But not well because the knob had one of those circles with a divot in the middle of it, one that he could use his thumbnail or a coin to turn.

No coins handy, he used his nail.

Approximately two seconds later, he was in the bathroom, holding Rebecca as she sobbed. His heart settled. No, it wasn't where he *wanted* to be. He definitely didn't want to be the cause of her tears.

Yet, he also knew there was nowhere else he would ever be.

No matter what Rebecca seemed to think.

———

"You should have left," she said into his chest, what felt like an eternity later. The heartrending sobs had stopped, and her voice was hoarse. "You should *still* leave."

Carefully, he leaned back, cradling her jaw in both hands and tilting her head so her eyes met his. "I thought we talked about this," he said. "I love you, Rebecca. Every part you've shown me willingly and all the pieces I still have to coax out underneath."

"I'm—"

"Perfect."

She shook her head.

"How about perfect for me?" he said, voice edging into cheesy game show host, complete with waggling brows.

Her sigh was put-upon, but at least amusement had crept into her eyes.

"This is a lot," he said. "I get it. We skipped about ten steps from friendship to lovers tonight, and I gave you too much. I should have waited—"

"You shouldn't have to do anything!" she screeched, pushing jerkily at his chest and climbing to her feet. "You shouldn't have to adjust just because I might have a freakout and lock myself in the fucking bathroom. You should be able to be you, to express your emotions, and I should be able to take them."

Ah.

The crux of her anxiety.

"And how many first dates have you been on where your date declares his love for you, huh?" He stood, took her hand when she would have turned away. "I'm guessing none." A beat. "Or at least under a dozen."

"Gabe," she snapped. "I'm being serious."

"I know, sweetheart." He tugged her close. "And I know this isn't a joke, but it's also not the end of the world. People make mistakes and go too fast or freak out or argue and run off. That's called being *human*." Fingers threading into the silk of her hair, he went on, "You once told me you weren't broken. I think you meant it at the time, but"—his tone went careful—"I'm not sure you actually believe that as much as you want to."

Her eyelids slammed closed, a long sigh escaping her lips. "My parents," she eventually said. "It wasn't healthy, you already know that. But what you can't understand it that my dad spent close to two decades accommodating, changing himself so that my mom wasn't triggered, so she didn't shut down and . . ." Another sigh, this time eyes opening. "Do what I just did. You're not my emotional shield, Gabe. I have to be able to handle these things on my own."

"But if we're in a relationship, why should you have to?"

"It's not that simple. You can't be my crutch."

"Why not?" he pressed. "Why can't I be one with this? There will come a time where I will need the same help back, and you'll bolster me then. Life isn't always transactional. Sometimes someone gives more, but then things shift and change and things even out."

Her shoulders curved forward slightly. "And if they don't even out? If you don't need me in the same way I need you?"

"Then you find other ways to take care of me," he said. "I'm a horrible cook, maybe it's meals—"

"You'd become vegan?"

"I'm mostly there anyway, and if becoming vegan meant getting to eat your cooking day in and day out, I'd do it in a heartbeat."

She placed her palm over his heart. "But do you *want* to?"

Gabe covered her hand, struggling to make her understand. He didn't give two shits about eating meat or not, and it was a fucking lame example, but he also knew what she was getting at. And it was less veganism and more concern for their future.

He also knew he would never be able to fully assuage those fears.

At some point, Rebecca would have to decide if she was willing to dip her toe over the line.

"I can't have you living half a life for *years*," she said. "Until you hit your limit and then finally leave—"

As if him leaving was already a foregone conclusion.

Fuck.

He'd missed that, too.

Not just a fear of replicating her parent's unhealthy relationship, but also a fear of abandonment. Because both her mom and dad had left her, albeit in different ways. Unfortunately, Gabe didn't have a magic solution to cure that particular fear—especially when the only true way to resolve it was time and patience and proving he wouldn't leave her, too.

Which left the anxiety.

And the fact that this woman didn't understand how truly strong she was. Not that he was any better. He'd ignored the signs at first, having been so distraught by her physical resemblance and personality similarities to Maggie—

*Fucking blinders.*

Mandy could be a pain in his ass, but she'd been damned right about that unique character flaw . . . and had not let him hear the end of it since. But when he'd finally pulled his head out of his ass, he'd truly seen Rebecca.

Yes, she had anxiety and was quiet and often reserved, especially with those she didn't know well. Yes, she didn't like speaking in front of groups or going to new places.

But. She. Went.

She spoke.

She came to work and did her job. She went to therapy, tried new places, gave presentations.

She fucking lived her life and lived it well.

*That* was worth celebrating.

But how to convince her? He couldn't. *She* needed to see that. "You're not your mom."

Her shoulders stiffened.

"You're not your mom."

A jerk of her head.

"*You're not your mom.*"

A tear trickled down her cheek, the glistening trail highlighted by the brightness of the bathroom. But no matter how much light was in the room, none of it was getting through the darkness of Rebecca's mind.

"It doesn't matter what I say, does it?" he asked quietly.

Silence.

Long, agonizing silence that sliced him straight in his gut.

Then finally, her lips parted, a tiny puff of air escaping, words following in its wake.

Unfortunately, they weren't the words he was desperate to hear.

"I can't be what you need me to be, Gabe."

"What I need is for you to be *you*."

Another tear escaped, slowly creeping down her pale cheek. "Maybe you think that's true now, but—"

It was the *but* that made him step back.

"I'm an adult," he reminded her. "I can make my own decisions, and I'm fully aware of what I can handle."

"I know," she said. "But you said earlier, I would find my own ways to take care of you." She swallowed. "This is my way."

Fucking hell. His pulse was pounding in his throat, anger and the fear of not having her in his life, mixing with the complete and utter helplessness he felt knowing he was losing her. He'd just had the best night of his life, and she was standing in front of him, just slipping through his fingers. "This isn't taking care of me," he said. "It's pushing me away because you're too fucking scared to take a chance on something that is real and important and might mean more to both of us than *anything* else in our lives."

She didn't react to his biting tone except to lightly brush her fingers down his jaw. "I've enjoyed being your friend," she said softly, "I'll miss it when I just have you as a coworker again."

As though it were a certainty.

*Fuck.*

He spun away, slammed a hand through his hair, probably disheveling the locks and not giving one fucking damn. This was agonizing. "Why won't you let me love you?"

A hand on his shoulder, burning his bare skin. "I can't," she whispered. "I can't do that to you."

Gabe's chin dropped to his chest, the inevitably of the argument sinking in.

"I hope you find what you need."

He turned and left the bathroom, shell-shocked at how incredibly quickly things had unraveled. Thirty minutes before, he'd been in the best place of his life. Now . . . his insides felt shredded, his heart smashed to a pulp.

And it was all supposedly for his own good.

Rebecca just didn't understand that everything that was good in his life revolved around her and without *her*—

Fucking torture.

But nothing he said would change her mind, would make her grasp the absolute certainty of his emotions.

So, there was nothing else to do.

Except, pull on his clothes, step into his shoes, and leave, knowing that he would never, *ever* be the same.

Such was the power of Rebecca.

# Eighteen

Rebecca

She'd just sat down with a bowl of oatmeal she had absolutely no intention of eating when her phone rang.

It was her broken heart that made her pick it up without looking at the screen.

Because her heart and brain were connected, right?

Unfortunately for her, that was the truth. Also unfortunate was the two organs were arguing for the entirety of the day about how it had been necessary to let Gabe go—her brain—but not liking it in the least and lambasting her for her decision—her heart.

She hadn't realized how much she loved Gabe until he'd left her apartment after quietly getting dressed, after softly reminding her to lock her door, even though she'd just eviscerated them both. He'd managed to get in deep, and she was hurting them both by breaking things off between them, but she also knew the call was the right one. He deserved someone—

Ugh.

Her phone buzzed in her hand, and she swiped a finger across the screen, answering the call and putting it on speakerphone.

"Rebecca."

The cell clattered to her kitchen counter.

"*Rebecca?*" came her sister's impatient voice.

"I'm here," she said. "Sorry, my hands were full, and I dropped the phone." Partial lie, because only *one* hand was occupied with oatmeal paraphernalia, but Sandra didn't need to know that.

"If your hands were full, why did you take the call?"

Tone condescending? Check.

Ice lacing the edges of her words? Double-check.

Continuing to talk without bothering to wait and listen to Rebecca's explanation? Priceless.

"You've been avoiding talking to me," Sandra said. "Why? Are you still seeing your therapist?"

Considering that she had been going to the same therapist for near on a decade now, the question was mute, but Rebecca answered anyway. "I'm still seeing Dr. Patel. Thanks for asking. What's new with you?"

Silence.

Cute.

Then, "How often?"

She shouldn't answer. First, it wasn't her sister's business or responsibility to make sure she was still going to therapy. But also, it wasn't for Sandra to know how often she was going.

Except, Rebecca had been down this track before.

It meant she either hopped on the train to its final destination or derailed the engine and dealt with the extended time and effort to right all of its cars.

Hence, she answered.

"Once a month."

"I think you should see her more," Sandra said. "You don't sound like yourself."

The space between her shoulder blades itched, or maybe that was just her finally growing a spine, because for the first time in a long time, she snapped back at her sister. "I think you should get a life so you can stop living mine."

"I—"

Rebecca shoved a spoonful of oatmeal in her mouth, not bothering to wait until she was done chewing to continue. Impolite, she knew, but this was more important than table manners.

"I love you, Sandra, but I'm serious. This is too much. You call me too much—"

"You're my sister. We should be talking—"

"I would *love* to talk to you," she snapped, throwing her hands up even though Sandra couldn't see them. "I would *love* to have a conversation with my sister about what's happening at her job or with her dating life or what show she's bingeing on Netflix. The only problem is that the only thing *she* wants to talk about is how fucked up I am and how much more therapy I should be getting."

Teeth clinking together, Rebecca stood and paced away.

"You don't sound—"

"I sound *fine!*" she shouted. "I'm finally living my life"—if being heartbroken was what she could call living it—"and I don't need to be in therapy all the time anymore. I'm not Mom!"

Her chest heaved when she finished talking . . . okay, *shouting*, her breaths coming short and rapid.

Her sister, however, was completely silent.

For a long time.

Long enough for Rebecca to cram another bite of oatmeal into her mouth. Not that she could taste it.

"This isn't like you."

She sucked in a deep breath, released it slowly. Gabe had transformed her, giving her the patience and support to find the strength to peel off the many layers of veneer and expose her true self to the world.

"Maybe you don't really know me," she said quietly. "I'm actually—"

"I'm your older sister. I *know* you."

More of that true self shone through. "Look, Sandra, I know you're older, and I understand that you lost out on a lot of fun during your college years by being forced to look after me when mom and dad were having their issues—"

"Dad didn't have—"

"Neither of them were innocent," she said firmly. "But this isn't about them"—her voice rose when Sandra began to talk over her again—"this is about *us*. I get you needed to be a mom to me when ours was out of commission. I understand what a sacrifice it was and am so beyond appreciative."

Sandra snorted.

"That being said," Rebecca continued. "I'm a grown-up now. I don't need another adult making unilateral decisions for me and my life."

As the words came out of her mouth, a feeling of dread bubbled up in her chest.

Wasn't that exactly what she'd done to Gabe?

*Fuck.*

But she couldn't focus on that in this moment. She needed Sandra to understand this way of interacting wasn't healthy for either of them.

"I'm just suggesting—"

Four months—hell, four *days* ago, she wouldn't have been able to stand up to her sister. But today, she found she had the strength. Because of Gabe, because of her own growth. It was as if he'd held up a mirror, one that only displayed who she was deep inside.

And deep inside, she was strong.

"Yes, I know. You're looking out for me. The trouble is, you're still doing it like a parent." A beat. "I need a sister."

Sandra was quiet for so long that Rebecca actually glanced down at her cell's screen to make sure she hadn't hung up.

"I'm not sure that *is* what you need."

Irritation welled. "Okay, you win, Sandra. Be what you want to be, but know that I'm not doing this anymore."

"That's not exactly fair, Rebecca."

"Maybe not," she said. "But fair doesn't factor in here. I'm telling you what I need, and that's a sister, not a mom. It's up to you if you want that role."

"I'm eighteen years older than you."

"Congratulations."

"I don't know why you're being like this."

"What? Strong? Or going after what I want? Look in the mirror. You're part of me. You taught me how." She sighed. "The difference was I spent my whole life wanting to be like you but never having the courage to do so. That's changed."

"It's a man."

"It *is* a man," she said. "And it's also me."

"That's idiotic."

Rebecca shrugged, another pointless gesture her sister couldn't see. "It's the truth."

Sandra scoffed. "That's ridiculous. What did he do—?"

"I'm hanging up now," Rebecca said. "I hope you'll actually listen to me and not—"

"You're acting like a petulant—"

"Look. You want to talk about a gorgeous new pair of heels you bought or some screw up your intern made or even which couples will make it on *Love is Blind,* then I'm all ears."

"I don't even know what that is."

"And point missed." She sighed again but kept her tone quiet and firm. "Be my sister, Sandra. Please, just find a way to be that."

Rebecca hit the end button.

Immediately her cell began to ring again.

She silenced it, picked up her bowl and took it to the sink, setting it carefully into the stainless-steel basin. That was when her hands began shaking, then her knees, then her breaths.

Slowly, she sank to the tile floor and for the second time that day, rested her head onto her thighs.

Holy shit.

Her sister. She'd actually said *all* of that to her sister.

Her first instinct was to grab her phone and call Gabe, to tell him that she'd stood up to Sandra for the first time in her life. He'd get how huge it was.

But he'd gone.

Because she'd pushed him away.

Right thing or not, that realization stung like hell.

It had been really fucking hard to convince him to go when her heart had been screaming at her to stop, to beg him to forgive her for putting them both through it, to stop the madness and confess her love for him.

She hadn't fully grasped exactly how much agony she was going to be in without Gabe in her life. Not until that moment.

Until she wanted him to pull her into his arms, to hug her close in celebration, to see the pride shining in his eyes that she'd stood up for herself.

But she couldn't have that.

She had finally found her strength.

And she was alone.

# Nineteen

Gabe

The arena was hopping.

Seventeen thousand Gold fans all thrilled by the way their team was playing—up by five goals—and showing their approval by cheering loudly.

Brit, shoulder back to normal, had started the game by making an incredible save off a broken down play in their own zone that had meant she'd suddenly been alone in the net with two of the opposing players bearing down on her.

The team had rallied for her, scoring four quick goals.

And Coop, freshly returned from his concussion and rib rehab, had scored three of them. The forward was in top shape, almost a blur on the ice as he moved with and away from the puck, dodging hits while throwing his own, battling in the corners and along the boards, passing and moving and just working really hard.

That was part of what made him such a good addition to the team.

He wasn't lazy, he had a great attitude, and he loved to play.

Needless to say, he'd slid right into his new team without any issues, and the Gold were lucky to have him.

And finally, the roster was back to normal, the team was healthy, and they were about to secure a few much-needed points to keep them in the running for the top spot in the Western Conference.

Normally, Gabe would eat this stuff up, loving that the team was coming together at exactly the right time, that he'd played some small part in that.

Tonight, however, he could barely stay focused on the game.

Rebecca.

She hadn't come into the arena that day. Not that he'd really expected her to, especially with all that had happened between them. Her job was largely based on a normal Monday to Friday schedule, since she didn't travel with the team. Also, the second phase of the diet plan had been rolled out and well-established by this point in the season so she didn't need to pull extra hours. Mostly, she'd been on maintenance for the last few weeks, helping injured players by adding foods to promote healing, adjusting meal plans for newfound food sensitivities, changing up calorie intake if players needed to increase or decrease their weight and muscle mass.

Still, she was *always* at the arena for home games, typically doing paperwork in her office, occasionally drifting down to the PT suite to check in on the guys rehabbing.

Tonight she wasn't.

Because of him.

He sighed. *Fuck.*

A whistle drew his attention to the ice and a group of players scuffling with each other near the crease.

Brit was smart and grabbed her water bottle and skated away from the mass of punching, squirming bodies. Though—Gabe grinned—she did give one of the opposing players a shove as she did so.

The linesmen broke up most of the scrums, but two

continued throwing punches, gaining space as they broke into a full-blown fight. Blue landed a few solid hits to the other player but took a glancing strike off his mouth. That would require some doctoring, no doubt about it.

Twenty seconds later, the linesmen had gotten between them. He shepherded Blue to the bench rather than the box because blood was dripping down his chin.

Gabe adjusted his gloves as he stepped to the side so Blue could walk down the hall. They would move out of sight of the cameras, assess and clean the wound then slap on some glue and butterfly bandages, if necessary, before returning Blue to the game.

Blue grabbed the towel Gabe held out and strode down the black mats that protected the edges of his skates from being dulled by the concrete of the arena floor. Gabe started to follow him then remembered that the supply bag he had in the hall was almost out of glue because of an earlier repair job they'd needed to do on Max.

He heard the whistle signaling the puck was going to be dropped as he spun back around and headed to the bench, bending to snag his bag stowed behind it.

Skates crunched on the ice as play began, voices rising as the teams jumped into motion, needing to communicate loudly enough to be heard over the crowd as well as the crack of sticks and noise of bodies colliding.

Gabe had straightened, bag in hand when he heard it.

The slightest *pop* of a puck being deflected.

There was an unfortunate thing about NHL players, about their game moving so quickly. While it was exciting, that speed was also dangerous.

Gabe didn't have time to react, to move or shift to the side.

One second the puck was safely on the ice.

The next, it was flying at his head.

# Twenty

Rebecca

The Gold game was on in the background as she alternated between working on her latest blog post and summaries of the chapters she wanted to write for her book on nutrition. As of that morning her initial proposal had been accepted, and the advance was safely ensconced in her checking account.

Exciting news she wanted to share with Gabe.

Exciting news she *couldn't* share with Gabe.

So, she'd done the next best thing, put on the game, hoping to hear the announcers say his name or catch a glimpse of him on camera as he tended to the players on the bench.

Typically, she did watch the team play, wanting to know who was skating well, who looked particularly winded after a game and might need their food plan adjusted.

But the team was up by five goals and she'd zoned out a bit, tinkering with her chapter on foods that boosted aerobic recovery time.

The whistles and shouting drew her focus, and she winced as Blue took a hard punch to the face. She didn't care what the guys said about adrenaline and heat of the moment, getting socked in the face really had to hurt.

Blue skated straight to the bench instead of the box, which meant he was bleeding and would need—

Her lungs turned to ice.

Gabe.

Fuck, he was so gorgeous standing there, alert and ready to help Blue. His hair was mussed, dark stubble on his jaw, and—

Her heart hurt.

She'd set him free, but she didn't think she could go about her day-to-day work, seeing him, just being friends with him, and survive. The book advance meant she had some savings, maybe she could find another sports team to—

Her eyes had drifted down to her laptop screen when play had begun again, but then she heard the tone of voice change on the TV announcer, concern lacing it, the noises of the game completely cut off.

Gut sinking, her eyes shot to the television, but instead of video of an injured player on the ice, it was a shot of the bench.

She was on her feet in an instant, laptop dropping to the rug, throat collapsing.

The camera shifted, moving from a pair of boots she knew too well to a body she'd learned every inch of the night before, up to a face that had gentled every time it looked down at her.

Gabe.

Eyes closed, completely prone, a growing puddle of blood surrounding him.

One instant and everything changed.

Fear of what she would do to him morphed into fear of what she would do *without* him.

Then, for once in her fucking life, she stopped thinking of all the ways this decision could go horribly wrong. Instead, she just grabbed her purse and sprinted out of her apartment.

# TWENTY-ONE

GABE

He groaned and reached a hand up to carefully probe his face, feeling like he'd been run over by a truck, rather than being grazed by a deflected puck.

"No touching."

Mandy.

Disappointment curled through him when he heard his friend's voice. Not because he wasn't relieved she was there patching him up, but because it wasn't Rebecca.

"How bad is it?"

"Laceration to your scalp," she said, shifting his head gently to the side. "It's still bleeding like hell, but it's not deep."

"From the puck?"

"Nope." She swapped towels. "From unluckily hitting your head on the corner of the bench as you went down."

"Fuck," he muttered.

"Good news is you'll have a nice bruise to match Blue's on your jaw," she said lightly and carefully probed his mouth, "but you didn't lose any teeth."

He started to push up. "I have to get back to the game."

She shook her head. "Cameron's got it. There are only five minutes left in the third. You, my friend, have a one-way ticket to the hospital."

"No—"

"Arguments," Mandy chimed in. "That's right. Good job following your own treatment plan you designed for players who get knocked out." She gestured to someone while still talking. "So, you can either let us help you to your feet so we can walk you to my car, and I'll drive you to the hospital. *Or* you can argue, and I'll have them bring the stretcher out and hog-tie you to it for your ambulance ride."

He made a face but knew better than to draw this out any longer. "Car," he grunted and pushed to his feet.

The arena erupted into cheers, the guys on the bench calling out encouragements as they tapped their sticks on the ice and boards.

Embarrassing as hell.

But also kind of nice.

Still, he was thankful Mandy stood with him, keeping the towel to his scalp and wrapping an arm around his waist when he staggered. Blane came to his other side, the burly player helping Gabe down the hall and into a wheelchair.

"Got him, love," Mandy murmured, pressing a kiss to Blane's lips. "Thanks."

Gabe grunted again, not happy about the wheelchair, but also knowing it was a long walk to the parking lot.

"I'll be there as soon as I can," Blane said.

"I know." She patted his jaw, and the gesture added acid to the already open wound on his heart when it conjured the memory of Rebecca's hand on *his* jaw.

Fuck, how was he going to do this, be with all of the ridiculously happy couples while knowing that he'd just narrowly missed out on *his* chance at that?

Pathetic. Devastating. *Agony.*

Knowing the reality of no Rebecca was his future hurt a hell of a lot more than his head, that was for damn sure.

"Here," Mandy said, grabbing his hand and putting a fresh towel in it. She brought his arm up so he could put pressure to the wound as she pushed.

Blue lightly punched his arm as they moved by him, one of the physicians from the team assessing his injury. "Nice wheels," he called.

"I'm never going to hear the end of this, am I?" he muttered.

"Probably not."

"Awesome."

"Are you grouchy because of the forthcoming teasing or because of a certain beautiful redhead?"

The teasing.

Fuck, who was he kidding? Definitely the redhead.

Still, he just adjusted the towel and said, "None of your business."

"Redhead."

"Shut up."

"Did you blow it?"

"Mandy," he sighed. "Didn't you ever hear the old idiom, *never pester a man with a head injury?*"

"Clearly not." She stopped outside the training suite and dashed in to grab her purse and car keys then began pushing him double time to the parking lot. "Because the head injury means it's the *perfect* time to get the truth out of you."

"Cruel."

"Nosy," she corrected, throwing on the brake before softening her teasing. "I want you to be happy, Gabe."

He heaved himself out of the wheelchair, keeping the towel in place as she helped him into the passenger's seat of her car. "I love her, Mandy."

She froze. "Oh." A huge smile growing on her face, she declared, "That's great!"

If he could have shaken his head without it hurting like a

mother, he would have, but Mandy knew him well enough by now to read between the lines.

"Rebecca will come around."

"I don't think so."

"She's come out of her shell the last months because of *you*."

"Not me," he said. "That was her."

"Maybe, but you helped her find the courage to do so."

"It's not enough."

"Gabe—"

"Please leave it"—he sighed—"Tomorrow, you can interrogate me further. Today, can you just drive?"

She was quiet for a long moment, but eventually, she nodded, rounded the hood, and got in.

Then she just drove.

# TWENTY-TWO

REBECCA

S he went to the arena first, which had been her initial error, then the wrong hospital, which had been Cameron's. The assistant trainer had been misinformed and Rebecca had been so worried she hadn't questioned it and by the time she'd realized—after arguing with the staff at the county hospital and driving an hour both ways through city traffic—she finally arrived at the right place.

Rebecca barreled out of her car, rushing to the front doors, and nearly mowing down Mandy as she came out of a sliding door, cell pressed to her ear.

"No, Allison," she said into the cell, steadying Rebecca with a hand on her shoulder. "Blane decided to *organize.* The extra diapers are in the gray cabinet to the right of the crib." A beat. "Right. Great. Thanks again for staying later than we'd planned. Blane will probably beat me home."

They exchanged a few more words before saying goodbye and hanging up.

"Hey," Mandy said, stowing her cell away. "I thought you would be here earlier."

Her friend's tone was laced with disappointment.

"I missed you at the arena," Rebecca told her. "Then Cameron said you took him to County and—" She shook her head. "Never mind that. Is he okay?"

Mandy tucked their arms together and walked them to the doors. "He's sleeping, waiting on results from a CT. Hit his head when he went down."

"I saw a lot of blood," she said.

"Scalp wounds bleed a lot. He only needed glue and a couple of stitches."

"O-okay." She released a shaky breath. "I-I—" Her chin dropped to her chest. "I fucked up."

Mandy chuckled lightly. "That's often a universal theme in finding your way to love."

"I worry that I'm going to bog him down, that's he's going to say all of my idiosyncrasies are cute and funny now, but at some point, he's going to get tired of them. That it's going to be too much and he'll . . ."

"Leave?"

Her heart pulsed. "Yeah."

Mandy dropped her head to Rebecca's shoulder. "Welcome to the club, girlfriend. You fight falling in love, but despite your best efforts to stay safely inside your protective armor, Gabe finds a way through anyway." Since that was an accurate description of the previous four months, Rebecca didn't argue as they made their way onto the elevator. "And Gabe's been all in from the moment he realized what you were to him, what you *could* be. He goes too fast, skips too many steps the moment he sees that you're tentatively ready to move forward. But he's like that, isn't he? Fearlessly moving forward despite any obstacle in his place."

Rebecca released a long, slow breath. "Yes."

Mandy pressed the button for the third floor. "So, what you have to decide here and now is if you're willing to accept him for his faults along with all the rest of it—the gentleness, the little chocolates and tea we've all been seeing him leave you on your desk, the way his smile changes when you're in the room. He's loyal, he loves you, and he won't stop no matter how hard you push him away." Mandy touched her arm. "But he does wear those blinders, and when he's wearing them, a bull in a china shop has nothing on him." The elevator doors opened with a ding. "You have to accept him for the flaws *and* the good things. Just as he's accepted you—"

"I—"

Mandy turned to face her, dropping her hands onto Rebecca's shoulders. "But what you really have to do is find the courage to believe that he's not going to leave you."

Rebecca's breath caught, tears welling in her eyes. "Mandy—"

Her friend hugged her tight. "I know, babe. That's the hard part for girls like us." Her voice dropped to a whisper. "But it's also the *best* part because when you find a man who's the other half of your soul, you know he'll always be there to catch you."

"You make it sound easy," she said, hugging Mandy back.

"Fuck no, it's not. That first step is absolutely terrifying." She dropped her arms. "It's just that every step after it gets easier— until you're not hovering on the edge, barely dipping your toes over, but launching yourself over the cliff, knowing he'll catch you."

"I—"

Mandy pointed to a door halfway down the hall. "He's in there." She nudged Rebecca that way. "Take the leap, babe. Be brave and. Just. Take. That. Leap."

Rebecca sucked in a breath, released it slowly, and with Mandy's words in her ear, pushed through into Gabe's room.

# TWENTY-THREE

## GABE

He was glued and stitched, his head was pounding, and he was annoyed at having to stay for a CT he thought was unnecessary, but he couldn't argue about it because he'd made the freaking protocol and disobeying it would set a bad example.

The first was his fault.

The second was Mandy's.

She was a great mom, and mostly because she had the whole mom guilt down. Not hard when she'd had a whole hockey team and support staff to practice on.

His snort made a pulse of pain lurch through his jaw, but he ignored it. He had very important other things to do. Like stare at his cell phone and wonder longingly if he should call Rebecca.

Just in case she heard something and was worried.

They were still friends, and friends did that, right?

And also, he really wanted to hear her voice.

He'd just slid his finger across the screen in what was probably the brain injury equivalent to drunk dialing, when the door to his room flew open. He glanced up, expecting Mandy, but instead—

Rebecca.

With pale, tear-streaked cheeks and shaky steps.

"Are you—" he began.

She jerked her head and ran across the room, launching herself into his bed and making him wince. But then she was in his arms and hugging him tight, and it was all fucking worth it.

"I'm so sorry."

"Baby," he whispered. "It's—"

"No," she said and pushed up. "I'm sorry I hurt you. I'm sorry I panicked. You and I both know that it's not the first or last time something like that will happen, but it still wasn't fair. I should have—" Her released breath was frustrated and staccato. "The truth is, it wasn't just the anxiety. I was scared because . . ."

"You don't want me to leave like your dad."

"Yes." She sighed again. "No. Or, fuck, yes *that* but also . . . you mean more to me than any other person *ever* has, and I just knew I was going to screw it up."

"Honey—"

She pressed a finger to his lips. "I *knew* that. The only difference is that now I also know you will, too." He laughed then winced, and she immediately tried to jump off the bed. "Oh no, your head. I'm—"

"I'm fine," he said, grabbing her by the waist and keeping her close. "Also, yes, I'm sure I'll mess up. *Many* times. The difference is that I'll do my best to make it up to you and then never do it again." She stopped fighting his hold, staring down at him with wide green eyes. "We're not your parents. Or anyone else, for that matter. We're just us. And we can find our own brand of happy, one that's perfect for *us*."

"I—" She touched his uninjured cheek, hesitating long enough that his gut was twisting itself in knots before she spoke again. "I know there are no guarantees in life, but that's the best damn offer I've ever heard."

He relaxed, pulling her close. "Killing me, sweetheart."

"I love you, Gabe. For a while now." She gently touched his

mouth with hers. "Even when I was too scared to admit it to myself."

His lips curved. "It's because I'm totally loveable."

She smacked him and he stole her mouth in a kiss that stung his injured cheek, but one that was the best ever anyway.

Because she'd come to him, because when things had come to a head, she'd pushed through.

For him.

So nothing else mattered.

"I love you, sweetheart," he murmured, when they broke apart.

"I love *you*." She rested her chin on his shoulder. "Now, how soon can we get you out of here?"

"As soon as the pain in the ass who ordered me to have a CT comes back with the results."

She frowned. "And who's that?"

"Me."

Her laughter carried him through the hour it took to get the results.

Just like it would carry him through the next seventy years.

# Epilogue

## Rebecca, One Year Later

She could do this. She could do this. She could—
Who the fuck was she kidding?
She totally could *not* do this.

*This* being book promotion. Major book promotion because her diet book was selling incredibly well after the guys on the team and her friends—yes, her *friends*, she was part of a group of awesome friends and those friends had her back to the nth degree. They'd recommended her book to friends, to fellow athletes, to a few B-list celebrities.

And now she was here.

In New York and about to be interviewed on a huge morning show, after which she'd be whisked off to a bookstore and be signing books.

Here, also being hiding in the bathroom stall at said morning show because her liaison with the publisher had told her that every seat was full, and standing room only was full, and that people were waiting outside on the sidewalk.

To meet her.

Her.

What the fuck was happening?

She'd come a long way in a year, was doing things she'd never thought possible. But this was just too much. Resting her head against the panel of the bathroom stall, she crouched on the floor next to the row of sinks, and took slow and steady breaths as she resisted the urge to pull out her cell and call Gabe.

He was busy with the team, overseeing a long homestand.

He had responsibilities.

He—

Lies.

She'd changed and become more confident over the last year and a half of being friends and more with Gabe. Her anxiety was manageable, almost more so because she had someone at her side who loved her without reservation and . . .

She didn't want Gabe to think she was weak.

He'd offered to come, but it was a busy time for the Gold, the typical pile-up of injuries and treatments as the long season took its toll. She didn't want her little book to take away from that.

But her little book wasn't so little anymore.

And neither was her anxiety.

Sweat trickled down her spine, her gut churned, her heart was pounding . . . and still her fingers refused to call him.

Too early in California.

Too—

"Stubborn as ever."

Rebecca gasped, her cell slipping from her fingers, but luckily Gabe was faster. He darted through the gap in the door and grabbed it before it hit the floor. A second later, he'd shoved it into his pocket and pulled her into his arms.

Warm. Pine and sandalwood drifting up to her nose. Immediately, she relaxed. Pavlov had nothing on Gabe, especially when he was holding her tightly, his lips at her ear, his hand rubbing gently up and down her back.

"You weren't going to call me, were you?"

She didn't want to fight, not with him holding her like this, so she didn't answer.

He understood her non-answer anyway and huffed. "I love you, you knucklehead." Lightly, he tugged on a strand of her hair. "But you don't have to push through alone anymore, remember?"

Her teeth found the corner of her mouth, nibbled. "Yes, but—"

"Partners." He leaned back, touched her chest with two fingers then his. "We're in this together and when the woman I love has something huge happening in her life, I'm going to be there." He touched his lips to her cheek, probably in deference to the lipstick the makeup artist had painstakingly applied. "No matter what. Or how stubborn she's being about pushing me away."

"But the team—"

"Will be fine for one night," he murmured. "You're more important. They know that. *I* know that. The only one not clued in is—"

"Me." She sighed, guilt pulsing. "I'm sorry. I didn't mean to push you away."

"I know, baby," he murmured. "But it's also why I'm here, not letting you push me away." She winced, but he just cupped her cheek and waited until she met his eyes. "I love you. I know you don't mean to do it. But it also doesn't mean *I'm* not going to be a stubborn bastard by staying close."

Her mouth quirked. "You seemed to be really good at staying *close* before I left."

His hand slid down to her waist, fingers tickling over the top of her butt. "That's because—"

"I'm a pain in the ass?"

He pinched her rump lightly. "Yup. Quite literally."

"Hey!" She smacked his hands away, and they laughed, Gabe winding his arms back around her and pulling her back into his arms.

"You're going to do great," he murmured. "It's plant proteins and cashew cheese and—"

A knock came on the bathroom door. "Rebecca? We're ready for you," a voice called.

"Oh fuck," she whispered.

"You got this," Gabe said with utter confidence, his eyes filled with warmth and love as he stared down at her.

"I've got this," she said. "I've. Got. This."

"You do have this," he agreed.

They walked to the door, hand and hand. She pulled it open, smiled at the production assistant, and announced, "I'm ready."

At the stage door, she paused.

And lipstick be damned, she turned back to the man she loved with all her heart, the one who loved every single piece of her, flawed or not, and . . . she kissed him.

"I love you," she murmured, cupping his cheek for one brief moment.

Then she straightened her shoulders, lifted her chin, and strode onto the set.

It was time to profess her love of cashew cheese to the world.

———

## Coop

"So, in conclusion, you need to get your fucking head out of your fucking ass," Calle snapped into her cell phone. "Otherwise, I swear to fucking God I will never, *ever* talk to you again."

Coop had just exited the arena door, the entire team having gathered to watch their nutritionist and newfound best-selling author, Rebecca, on a national morning show promoting her book. The shy, quiet redhead was unassuming, but also a major reason the Gold were currently the number one team in the league. She'd come up with the diet plan the entire team was following and a major source of their increased energy and shortened injury recovery time.

He knew he, for one, had never felt better thanks to Rebecca and the rest of the training staff.

But another one of the reasons the team was doing so incredibly well was standing right in front of him, forehead pressed to her clenched fists, one of which still clutched her cell phone.

Calle Stevens, newest assistant coach for the Gold and former national team member. Tall for a woman and built, with strong thighs, shoulders, and arms that bespoke of the grace and fierce player she'd been on the ice. She might have blown out her knee, but that inner athlete never completely faded. Add in a head for the game that out thought most coaches twice her age and she had been a huge boon to the team when they'd picked her up.

She was also even.

That was the best description Coop could think for her. Never raised her voice, always ready with a smile or joke. Stern sometimes, yes. Tough, for sure. But she wasn't a yeller.

And after playing hockey from the time he was five, he'd been on plenty of teams with yellers.

Calle sighed and pocketed her phone, staring off into the distance for several long moments before sweeping her long brown hair back into a ponytail and turning to reenter the building.

Which was the moment that he realized he should have moved.

Coop should have gone when he'd stumbled onto the conversation that was obviously private because she'd stepped outside to take it.

But he hadn't because . . . well, Calle wasn't the type of person who screamed into cell phones, who took long, centering breaths before dashing her thumb under each eye, as though she was wiping away tears.

She didn't cry. She didn't yell. She—

Was staring right at him.

"Hey," she said, after a long moment, blinking the distance from her gaze, though he noticed she still focused on a point over his left shoulder and not on him. "You have a chance to review those tapes from Dani?" she asked.

Dani was their video coach and the woman was able to cut, prep, and send clips of games to the team's tables faster than most people could unlock their phones. Calle had asked her to send over a package the previous day and he'd watched them this morning. He nodded. "Yeah, thanks for that. I think it'll be helpful for me on the breakout. Especially against Tampa Bay."

Calle brushed a hand through her hair. "Good, good," she said distractedly.

He frowned. "Are you okay?"

"Hmm?" She finally met eyes. "Yeah. I'm great."

Except her tone was completely off.

"Calle," he said.

Anger edged into her expression, mouth opening, and Coop braced for some of the same pissed-off woman that he'd overheard on her call. But almost just as quickly, that fury faded and her pretty brown eyes filled with tears.

"I'm fine," she whispered. "I'll be fine."

"Who was on the phone?" he asked.

"Doesn't matter."

"*Calle.*"

"It doesn't." She shook her head brusquely, sucked in a breath.

Maybe he would have let it go, let *her* go as she walked by, kept things between them strictly professional.

But then he saw the tear.

Glistening in the morning light as it escaped the corner of her eye.

Without thinking, he caught her arm.

"You're not okay."

She shuddered to a stop when he touched her, not fighting

the grip, chin dropping to her chest. "No," she said, "you're right. I'm not okay."

"Who was on the phone?" he asked gently.

Her jaw went tight. "My ex."

Fury blazed through him. Tears. Sadness. Depression. He'd seen it before, had promised himself he would never let another woman in his world go through that. "Did he hurt you?" he growled.

A shake of her head. "Not like you're thinking." She sucked in a breath. "He broke my heart."

Coop's own heart twinged. "I'm sorry, Calle. That's—"

"Fucking stupid." Another tear joined the first, dripping down the pale skin of her cheek.

"It's not stupid to have loved someone," he said gently.

Her eyes went fierce. "It's incredibly stupid when the person who supposedly loves you right back doesn't give a damn that you're pregnant."

His jaw fell open, he knew it did.

But Calle? Even, gentle, *Calle* had gotten knocked up and—

"Yup," she said, brushing by him. "See? Really *fucking* stupid."

And without another word, she disappeared into the rink.

———

Thank you for reading! I hope you loved meeting Rebecca and Gabe as much as I loved writing them! The next book in the Gold Hockey series is COASTING.

**Calle Stevens wasn't what one would call a risk-taker.**
**She was steady. She was even. She was . . . pregnant.**

CLICK HERE TO READ COASTING>

And if you enjoyed CHECKED, you'll love the sexy, sweet, and close-knit Breakers Hockey crew. <u>The first book in the series,</u> <u>BROKEN, is now live!</u>

> *"It is sexy, hot, adorable and such a fun read. You will not*
> *be able to put this down!"* —Amazon Reviewer

**I'd brought him home thinking that for once in my life I would live a little.** Now weeks later...I was puking my guts up and had a pink stick with a plus sign on it declaring my future.

DOWNLOAD BAD NIGHT STAND FOR FREE HERE >

I so appreciate your help in spreading the word about my books, including sharing with friends! Please leave a review on your favorite book site!
You can also join my Facebook group, the Fabinators, for exclusive giveaways and sneak peeks of future books.

SIGN UP FOR ELISE FABER'S NEWSLETTER HERE:
https://www.elisefaber.com/newsletter

---

Want a free bonus story? Hate missing Elise's new releases? Love contests, exclusive excerpts and giveaways?
Then signup for Elise's newsletter here!
https://www.elisefaber.com/newsletter

---

And join Elise's fan group, the Fabinators https://www.facebook.com/groups/fabinators for insider information, sneak peaks at new releases, and fun freebies! Hope to see you there!

# GOLD HOCKEY SERIES

# GOLD HOCKEY

Did you miss any of the Gold Hockey books?
Find information about the full series here.
Or keep reading for a sneak peek into each of the books below!

**Blocked**
*Gold Hockey Book #1*
Get your copy at https://www.elisefaber.com/blocked

## BRIT

The first question Brit always got when people found out she played ice hockey was *"Do you have all of your teeth?"* The second was *"Do you, you know, look at the guys in the locker room?"*

The first she could deal with easily—flash a smile of her full set of chompers, no gaps in sight. The second was more problematic. Especially since it was typically accompanied by a smug smile or a coy wink.

Of course she looked. *Everybody* looked once. Everyone snuck a glance, made a judgment that was quickly filed away and shoved deep down into the recesses of their mind.

And she meant *way* down.

Because, dammit, she was there to play hockey, not assess her teammates' six packs. If she wanted to get her man candy fix, she could just go on social media. There were shirtless guys for days filling her feed.

But that wasn't the answer the media wanted.

Who cared about locker room dynamics? Who gave a damn whether or not she, as a typical heterosexual woman, found her fellow players attractive?

Yet for some inane reason, it *did* matter to people.

Brit wasn't stupid. The press wanted a story. A scandal. They were desperate for her to fall for one of her teammates—or better yet the captain from their rival team—and have an affair that was worthy of a romantic comedy.

She'd just gotten very good at keeping her love life—as nonexistent as it was—to herself, gotten very good at not reacting in any perceptible way to the insinuations.

So when the reporter asked her the same set of questions for the thousandth time in her twenty-six years, she grinned—showing off those teeth—and commented with a sweetly innocent "Could've sworn you were going to ask me about the coed showers." She waited for the room-at-large to laugh then said, "Next question, please."

–Get your copy at https://www.elisefaber.com/blocked

## Backhand
*Gold Hockey Book #2*
Get your copy at https://www.elisefaber.com/backhand

## SARA

"Sorry I messed up your sketch," he rumbled.

She nibbled on the side of her mouth, biting back a smile. "Sorry I stole your hand for so long."

He shrugged. "My mom's an artist. I get it."

Well, there went her battle with the smile. Her lips twitched and her teeth came out of hiding. If there was one thing that Sara had, it was her smile. It had been her trademark in her competition days.

Which were long over.

Her mouth flattened out, the grin slipping away. Time to go, time to forget, to move on, to rebuild. "Thanks," she said and extended a hand.

Then winced and dropped it when her ribs cried out in protest.

"You okay?" he asked, head tilting, eyes studying her.

"Fine." And out popped her new smile. The fake one. Careful of her aching side, she shrugged into her backpack. "I've got to go." She turned, ponytail flapping through the hair to land on her opposite shoulder.

"That—" He touched her arm. "Wait. I *know* I know you."

She froze. That was the second time he'd said that, and now they were getting into dangerous territory. Recognition meant . . . no. She couldn't.

There had been a time when *everyone* had known her. Her face on Wheaties boxes, her smile promoting toothpaste and credit cards alike.

That wasn't her life any longer.

"Thanks again. Bye." She started to hurry away.

"Wait." A hand dropped on to her shoulder, thwarting her escape, and she hissed in pain.

"Sorry," he said, but he didn't release her. Instead, he shifted his grip from her aching shoulder down to her elbow and when she didn't protest, he exerted gentle pressure until Sara was facing him again. "It's just that know I *know* you."

No. This wasn't happening.

"You're Sara Jetty."

Her body went tense.

*Oh God*. This was *so* happening.

"It's me." He touched his chest like she didn't know he was talking about himself, and even as she was finally recognizing the color of his eyes, the familiar curve of his lips and line of his jaw, he said the worst thing ever, "Mike Stewart."

Oh *shit*.

—Get your copy at https://www.elisefaber.com/backhand

## Boarding
### *Gold Hockey Book #3*
Get your copy at https://www.elisefaber.com/boarding

## MANDY

Hockey players had the *best* asses.

No pancake bottoms, these men—and *women*—could fill out a pair of jeans. She wanted to squeeze it, to nibble it, bounce a dime—

Mandy dropped her chin to her chest, losing sight of the Sorting Hat cupcakes she'd been pondering.

Blane with his yummy ass had a unique way of distracting her.

No, it wasn't even distraction, per se. He had *always* been able to get under her skin.

And that was very, very bad for her.

"Ugh," she said, tossing her phone onto her desk and standing, knowing that she wouldn't be able to sit still now.

Nope, she needed about forty laps in the pool and a good hard fu—

*Run*, her mind blurted, almost yelling at the mental voice of her inner devil. *A good hard run.*

Unfortunately, the cajoling tone wasn't completely drowned out. *Some sexy horizontal time with Blane would be more fun—*

But the rest of the enticing words were lost as the roar of the crowd suddenly penetrated through the layers of concrete. Her stomach twisted. Mandy could tell, even before her eyes made it to the television, that it wasn't in celebration of a goal or a good hit either.

This was fury, a collective of outrage.

She was on her feet the moment she saw the prone form lying so still face down on the ice.

Her gut twisted when she spotted the curving line of a numeral two on the back of the player's jersey.

"Not him," she said and the words were familiar, a sentiment she had whispered, had *prayed* a thousand times before. She needed the camera angle to shift, for her to be able to see more clearly *who* was hurt. "Not him."

Then Dr. Carter was on the ice and the player moved slightly, rolling away from the camera, giving a full shot of his back and the matching twos adorning his jersey.

*Fuck.* Not him. Not Blane.

And that was when she saw the pool of blood.

—Get your copy at https://www.elisefaber.com/boarding

### Benched
*Gold Hockey Book #4*
Get your copy at https://www.elisefaber.com/benched

## MAX

He started up the car, listening and chiming in at the right places as Brayden talked all things video game.

But his mind was unfortunately stuck on the fact that women were not to be trusted.

He snorted. Brit—the Gold's goalie and the first female in the NHL—and Mandy—the team's head trainer—would smack him around for that sentiment, so he silently amended it to: *most* women were not to be trusted.

There. Better, see?

Somehow, he didn't think they'd see.

He parked in the school's lot, walked Brayden in, and received the appropriate amount of scorn from the secretary for being thirty minutes late to school, then bent to hug Brayden.

"I'll pick you up today," he said.

Brayden smiled and hugged him tightly. Then he whispered something in his ear that hit Max harder than a two-by-four to the temple.

"If you got me a new mom, we wouldn't be late for school."

"Wh-what?" Max stammered.

"Please, Dad? Can you?"

And with that mind fuck of an ask, Brayden gave him one more squeeze and pushed through the door to the playground, calling, "Love you!" over his shoulder.

Then he was gone, and Max was standing in the office of his son's school struggling to comprehend if he had actually just heard what he'd heard.

A new mom?

Fuck his life.

—Get your copy at https://www.elisefaber.com/benched

## Breakaway
*Gold Hockey Book #5*
Get your copy at https://www.elisefaber.com/breakaway

## BLUE

"Thanks for the ride."

"Try not to go out and get a fresh bimbo to ride tonight. I hear STIs on are the rise in the city."

Blue sighed, turned back to face her. "Really?"

She shrugged, smirk teasing the edges of her mouth, drawing

his focus to the lushness of her lips. "Just watching out for Max's teammate."

He rolled his eyes. "Not hardly."

"Okay, how about I'm trying to prevent you from spreading STIs to the female populace."

"I'm clean, and I'm smart," he told her. "Condoms all the way."

"Ew."

Except there was something about the way she said it that made Blue stiffen and take notice. Because . . . he stared into her eyes, watched as the pale blue darkened to royal, saw her lips part, and her suck in a breath.

Holy shit.

"You're attracted to me."

Her jaw dropped. "No fucking way," she said, too quickly, pink dancing on the edges of her cheekbones. "You're delusional."

Blue got close.

*Real* close.

Anna licked her lips.

And fuck it all, he kissed that luscious mouth.

—Breakaway, https://www.elisefaber.com/breakaway

**Breakout**
*Gold Hockey Book #6*
Get your copy at https://www.elisefaber.com/breakout

## PR-REBECCA

A fucking perfect hockey fairy tale.

Shaking her head, because she knew firsthand that fairy tales didn't exist outside of rom-coms and occasionally between alpha sports heroes and their chosen mates, Rebecca slipped through the corridor and stepped onto the Gold's bench.

Lots of dudes in suits—of both the boardroom *and* the hockey variety—were hugging.

On the ice. Near the goals. On the bench.

It was a proverbial hug-fest.

And she was the cynical bitch who couldn't enjoy the fact that the team she was with had just won the biggest hockey prize of them all.

"I knew you'd be like this."

Rebecca turned her focus from Brit, who was skating with the huge silver cup, to the man—no, to the *boy* because no matter how pretty and yummy he was, Kevin was still a decade younger than her—leaning oh so casually against the boards.

"Nice goal," she told him.

A shrug. "Blue made a nice pass."

And dammit, the fact that he wasn't an arrogant son of a bitch made her like him more.

She nodded at the cup. "You should go have your turn."

"I'll get mine," he said with another shrug.

She frowned, honestly confused. "You don't want—"

Suddenly he was in front of her on the bench, towering over her even though she was wearing her four-inch power heels. "You know what I want?"

Rebecca couldn't speak. Her breath had whooshed out of her in the presence of all that sweaty, hockey god-ness. Fuck he was pretty and gorgeous and . . . so fucking masculine that her thighs actually clenched together.

She wanted to climb him like a stripper pole.

"Do you?" he asked again when her words wouldn't come. "Want to know what I want?"

She nodded.

He bent, lips to her ear. "You, babe," he whispered. "I. Want. You."

Then he straightened and jumped back onto the ice, leaving her gaping after him like she had less than two brain cells in her skull.

The worst part?

She wanted him, too.

*Had* wanted him since the moment she'd laid eyes on the sexy as sin hockey god.

"Trouble," she murmured. "I'm in *so* much fucking trouble."

—Breakout, https://www.elisefaber.com/breakout

Coasting

Centered

Charging

Caged

Crashed

A Gold Christmas

Cycled

Caught

***Breakers Hockey (all stand alone)***

<u>Broken</u>

<u>Boldly</u>

<u>Breathless</u>

<u>Ballsy (April 26, 2022)</u>

***Love, Action, Camera (all stand alone)***

Dotted Line

Action Shot

Close-Up

End Scene

Meet Cute

***Love After Midnight* (all stand alone)**

Rum And Notes

Virgin Daiquiri

On The Rocks

Sex On The Seats

***Life Sucks Series* (all stand alone)**

Train Wreck

Hot Mess

Dumpster Fire

Clusterf*@k

FUBAR (March 29, 2022)

**Roosevelt Ranch Series (all stand alone, series complete)**

Disaster at Roosevelt Ranch

Heartbreak at Roosevelt Ranch

Collision at Roosevelt Ranch

Regret at Roosevelt Ranch

Desire at Roosevelt Ranch

**Phoenix Series (read in order)**

Phoenix Rising

Dark Phoenix

Phoenix Freed

**Phoenix: LexTal Chronicles (rereleasing soon, stand alone, Phoenix world)**

From Ashes

In Flames

To Smoke

**KTS Series**

Riding The Edge

Crossing The Line

Leveling The Field

Scorching The Earth

**Cocky Heroes World**

Tattooed Troublemaker

# About the Author

*USA Today* bestselling author, Elise Faber, loves chocolate, Star Wars, Harry Potter, and hockey (the order depending on the day and how well her team -- the Sharks! -- are playing). She and her husband also play as much hockey as they can squeeze into their schedules, so much so that their typical date night is spent on the ice. Elise changes her hair color more often than some people change their socks, loves sparkly things, and is the mom to two exuberant boys. She lives in Northern California. Connect with her in her Facebook group, the Fabinators or find more information about her books at www.elisefaber.com.

f facebook.com/elisefaberauthor

a amazon.com/author/elisefaber

BB bookbub.com/profile/elise-faber

O instagram.com/elisefaber

g goodreads.com/elisefaber

P pinterest.com/elisefaberwrite

www.ingramcontent.com/pod-product-compliance
Lightning Source LLC
Chambersburg PA
CBHW071120100726
47908CB00008B/2436